Full Figured 16:

Carl Weber Presents

Full Figured 16:

Carl Weber Presents

La Jill Hunt

and

Kamaryn Hunt

www.urbanbooks.net

Urban Books, LLC
300 Farmingdale Road, NY-Route 109
Farmingdale, NY 11735

ISBN 13: 978-1-64556-127-9
ISBN 10: 1-64556-127-5

First Trade Paperback Printing February 2022
Printed in the United States of America

10 9 8 7 6 5 4 3 2 1

Distributed by Kensington Publishing Corp.
Submit Orders to:
Customer Service
400 Hahn Road
Westminster, MD 21157-4627
Phone: 1-800-733-3000
Fax: 1-800-659-2436

Full Figured 16:

Carl Weber Presents

La Jill Hunt

and

Kamaryn Hunt

Married to a Duncan

by

La Jill Hunt

Chapter 1

"You all have full access to the community amenities: pool, clubhouse, and fitness center. Everything you need is in this folder, and you have my number if you need me," Charlene Bivins said as she extended the manila folder.

I smiled at the pleasant Realtor we'd spent most of the morning with. She was a nice-looking woman in her mid-forties who spoke with a heavy Southern accent. That accent was something I realized I'd have to get used to because it seemed that everyone we'd encountered since arriving in Houston two days ago had the same one. I was sure our New York accents sounded just as foreign to the native Texans as theirs did to me.

"Thank you so much, Charlene. We appreciate everything you've done for us." Junior, my husband, took the folder and shook Charlene's hand.

"It's been a pleasure, Mr. Duncan. Here are your keys. Oh, and the security company should be here shortly to make sure the alarm system is in place." Charlene held up two sets of keys.

"Actually, that won't be necessary. My family has a preferred company we deal with that we'll be using," Junior told her as he took the keys.

"Are you sure? The service is already included in your builder's contract, and the monthly service is free for the first six months." Charlene sounded confused by Junior's rejection. I was sure she thought she was doing us a favor, but little did she know, one thing my husband's family did not take lightly was their security. Even before marrying into the family, I'd quickly learned that being a Duncan meant being safe. And being safe meant having the right kind of protection.

"I'm positive," Junior assured her.

"Well, okay then. If you change your mind, just let me know." Charlene smiled as we walked her to the front door.

"You've been great, Charlene. Thank you so much," Junior told her.

"You've been a great client, Mr. Duncan. I gotta say, this is probably the easiest sale I've ever made." She looked over at me. "Congratulations again on your recent nuptials, and welcome to Texas."

I suppressed my initial reaction and instead gave a pleasant smile. "Thank you."

Charlene walked down the driveway and got into the Volvo station wagon with her photo and contact information displayed on the door. When she drove off, I turned to Junior.

"Sale?"

Junior shrugged. "Welcome home, baby."

I threw my arms around Junior's thick torso as he leaned down to kiss me. I didn't know what I'd done to deserve a man who loved me the way he did, but I was grateful. From the moment we met, the love between us was real. It was the thing that had allowed us to endure everything we'd had to in such a short period of time. I'd sworn off love forever after my first marriage to Charles, who changed his name to Brother X after converting to Islam. Eventually, Brother X became the leader of the Brotherhood, a murderous gang who specialized in street assassinations. His criminal activity landed him in jail, but he continued tormenting me from behind bars, especially after I tried to divorce him. It was Junior and his family who finally helped me become free.

"Junior, I can't believe you bought us a house," I gushed when our passionate kiss finally ended. "You don't think it's too soon though? I mean, what if we don't like it here?"

Junior shrugged. "We sell it and go back home or wherever you wanna go."

"You are amazing, do you know that?" I said, still in disbelief.

"You don't understand how hard I was praying during the walk-through. I was so focused on surprising you that it didn't dawn on me that there was a chance that you might not like it until we got here."

"I mean, I don't like it." I sighed.

"You don't?" He frowned.

"I love it. It's absolutely perfect, baby." I smiled and grabbed his hand.

The house was absolutely gorgeous. Four bedrooms, three bathrooms, with a game room, which Junior already claimed as his "mancave," and a state-of-the-art kitchen that I already imagined enjoying as I whipped up some of my favorite dishes and desserts. It wasn't too big, nor too small, especially since we'd already started talking about starting a family.

"Are you sure? Because, you know, we don't have to keep it. If you don't love it, we can find another one you want," Junior told me. "I want you to be happy."

"I am happy, Junior. I've been happy since the day we met, and it has nothing to do with a house. You make me happy no matter where we are. You already know that." I sighed.

"You're right. We're happy as long as we're together." He nodded and pulled me close. "But don't act like you haven't been dropping hints about being ready to move."

I couldn't help laughing. For the past two weeks, since moving to our new state of residence, we'd been staying at The St. Regis hotel in downtown Houston. As much as I loved the superior five-star accommodations of the governor's suite, including our butler service, there was only so much afternoon tea and eating in restaurants I could take. I was ready to enjoy our own space, not to mention that you could only be so loud while having hotel sex. I was ready to be *loud*.

"I haven't been that bad, have I?"

"You've definitely been dropping hints, that's for sure. The comment you made to the waiter the other night at dinner was quite obvious." He raised an eyebrow at me.

"What? My bread pudding is better," I said. "And I meant what I said—whenever I get into my own kitchen and make it, I'm gonna bring him some so he can taste it."

"Well, we got something else to make before you make that." Junior grinned.

"What's that?" I peered at him.

"A baby to put into one of those extra bedrooms." He playfully grabbed my ass.

I allowed him the feel, enjoying it myself, then swatted him away. "Aren't you putting the cart before the horse, sir?"

"How's that? I put a ring on it already." He lifted my left hand, which held my five-carat Asscher-cut diamond wedding ring.

"We gonna make our baby on the floor?" I asked.

"Of course not, unless that's where you wanna make it," he said, then pointed to the large moving truck heading toward us.

I watched as it turned into the driveway of our new home. "Wait, you already bought furniture?"

"Just a bed. Don't worry. Ma sent me pictures of the one you liked from your Pinterest, and I got it. The rest of the home is yours to do with as you wish, but I wanted to make sure we were prepared in case you were satisfied with the house," he said. "I figured you might wanna go ahead and christen our bedroom."

I took his hand and pulled him toward the door. "Junior Duncan, you have no idea."

Chapter 2

We didn't waste any time moving out of the hotel, but not before the high-tech smart-security system was in place and up to Junior's standard. He made sure there was full video surveillance of the entire house, inside and out, and motion sensors for all the doors and windows. The comprehensive system gave us access to every-thing—locks, garage door opener, lights, sirens, even the sprinkler system—from our phones via Wi-Fi.

"Baby, don't you think this is a bit much?" I asked as he showed me how to access everything from my phone.

"Nope, it's not." He shook his head.

"But isn't part of the reason we moved out here was so that you didn't have to live like this anymore?" I referred to the Duncan compound we'd left behind in New York where we lived with the rest of his family. They even had their own security detail.

"Well, technically, we moved so I could get a fresh start and start my own business," Junior reminded her. "But I'm still a Duncan, and now so are you."

Junior's parents, LC and Chippy Duncan, had done well for themselves with their car dealership, Duncan Motors. Secretly being one of the largest international narcotics dealers added to their fortune and was also the cause for the extreme security measures. Each of the Duncan siblings had a position within the business. Orlando was a brilliant scientist who created new prod-ucts for distribution. London, the older of Junior's two sisters, was married with children but recently began her own business ventures. Youngest brother Rio owned an upscale nightclub. Paris, Rio's twin, was the trouble-maker of the family who did more damage than good. The one who was most like his father was his brother Vegas, groomed to take over the Duncan family dynasty but unable to do so because he was currently behind bars and looked like he would be there for a while. For years, Junior had been relegated to be the "muscle" of the family. At six foot five and nearly 300 pounds, his size played a major part in his role in the Duncan empire. Now that he was married, he desired more. I had no problem sup-porting my husband, and I encouraged him to follow his dreams. So when he decided to use his love of cars and experience as a mechanic to start his own racing team, I encouraged him. Moving across the country was a new adventure for us, and I welcomed the opportunity for a fresh start for just the two of us.

"Okay, baby, if you think all of this is necessary, then better safe than sorry." I shrugged.

"Exactly." He winked. "Plus, I can see what your fine ass is doing when I'm not home."

"Two can play that game, sir. If you stalking me, I can stalk you too." I laughed.

"You already know the only thing you gonna catch me doing is either sleeping or watching *SportsCenter*. The same thing I do when you're here with me." Junior grinned.

He was right. My husband was crazy about me, and I was confident that spying on him was something I wouldn't have to do. Not only did he constantly affirm me verbally, but his actions were proof that he loved me. I made sure to reciprocate and that he knew where home was. Junior Duncan wasn't going anywhere.

"I am glad we got everything done and most of the house furnished. You know tomorrow is my big day." I snuggled beside him on the comfortable leather sofa that had been delivered a couple of days prior.

"You aren't nervous, are you?" He looked down at me. "You don't have to do this. Honestly, you know I prefer that you didn't."

"Junior, we've talked about this. I enjoy working, and I plan to do so until I have a reason not to. My job is fulfilling for me." I sighed. "And to answer your question, no, I'm not nervous. I'm excited more than anything. I've already met the doctors and other staff of the practice, and everyone seems cool. Already knowing Isis does make it a little easier for me. She's just as crazy as her sister."

Isis, my soon-to-be new coworker, was the sister of my best friend, Jasmine. Once she found out I was moving to Texas, she called and let me know that the office she worked for had an opening that she knew I'd be perfect for. One application and a single Zoom interview, and before we'd made it to the state, I was the new triage nurse at Houston Women's Wellness, one of the busiest OB-GYN clinics in the city. I was grateful not only to have a new job but also a friend in the area.

"I can't imagine anybody crazier than Jazz. I hope she ain't as man-hungry," Junior teased.

"My bestie is not man-hungry. She's just ready to love."

"She's ready to lust, that's what she is."

I playfully slapped Junior on the chest. He grabbed my hand and began kissing my fingers. It was a small gesture, but I found myself turned on. In one swift movement, I straddled him, enjoying the feel of his lips as they made their way along my wrist, up my arm, and finally to my collarbone.

"Mmmmm." A slight moan escaped me as I slipped my hand into his sweatpants and found what I was looking for. "Seems like you're the one ready for some lust."

"Damn right I am." He slipped my shirt over my head and proceeded to taste each and every inch of my body before making love to me on the floor. It felt good to be able to enjoy moments like this with no one else around. Having our own space was something I planned to enjoy for a long time. And I was looking forward to christening each and every room of our new home.

"You should just call and tell them you'll start tomorrow instead of today," Junior said the next morning as we both got dressed for work.

"I'm not doing that." I shook my head.

"I know you're tired. It's not like either one of us got any sleep last night."

"That wasn't my fault." I looked at him from the corner of my eye. "You're the one who wanted to live in Fort Knox, not me."

Most of our sleep the night before had been interrupted by the security system going off. It was so sensitive that the slightest movement would set it off: the AC unit turning on, a pillow falling off the bed, a raccoon in the backyard. At one point I told him to just disconnect the thing, but he refused.

"I promise I'll have it fixed today. As a matter of fact, I already texted the owner of the company, and they're sending someone out this morning." He added, "But I still plan on dropping you off."

"No, you don't have to do that, Junior. I can drive myself. Besides, I need to get used to the city," I told him, admiring my reflection in the full-length mirror. "How do I look?"

"You already know you look sexy as hell." He grinned.

"That's not quite the look I was going for, but I'll take the compliment." I laughed.

"Well, that's all I see when I look at you." He hugged me from behind.

Suddenly, the loud alarm rang out again. I eased from his arms and turned around. "Junior Duncan."

"I promise it'll be taken care of today, baby." He sighed and rushed to grab his cell phone to pull up the app for the security system. Seconds later, the noise finally stopped.

I noticed the time and saw that if I didn't hurry, I'd be late. "Baby, I love you but I gotta go."

Junior walked me to the brand-new Tesla I picked out sitting in the garage. "You sure you don't want me to drive you?"

"I'm positive." I kissed him, then hit the unlock button.

"I'll open the garage door for you," he volunteered, taking his phone out. He typed on the screen, but nothing happened. "Damn, this thing is tripping."

I clicked the traditional opener that was on the visor of my car, and the door lifted behind me. I smiled at Junior and said, "Don't worry, honey, I got it."

"Have a great day. I love you," he said.

"I love you too," I told him.

As I drove through the streets of our neighborhood, I noticed the moms pushing strollers as they walked or jogged on the sidewalks. I wondered if that would be me in the near future. Imagining myself as a suburbanite was so funny considering the fact that, not too long ago, I was living in Brooklyn.

My cell phone rang, and Isis's name and number appeared on the car's iPad display.

"Good morning," I answered.

"Hey, girl. I'm sure you're on your way," Isis responded. "I just wanted to let you know I was stopping at Starbucks and grabbing coffee."

"Thank you, because I'm definitely gonna need some this morning," I told her. "A sister had a long night."

"Please spare me. It's too early for me to be listening to the details of your and Junior's newlywed fun. You can share them when we go to lunch," Isis teased.

"I wasn't gonna tell you any details. You know I'm not like your sister. I don't kiss and tell."

"That chick tells everything, Lord knows: kissing, hugging, touching, loving." Isis laughed. "And it don't even be about her."

"Hold on now, I ain't gonna let you talk about my bestie like that." I laughed.

"We both know my sister runs her mouth. But I'll see you at the office."

"Okay, see you in a little while," I told her, then remembered I hadn't given her my order. "Isis, hold up."

"Yeah?"

"Can you please get me a—"

"Venti white mocha, no whip, with Stevia and almond milk, and a vanilla biscotti." Isis spit out my favorite Starbucks order before I could. "See, I told you Jazz tells everything."

"Damn, she really does." I laughed. As if she heard us talking about her, my best friend called at that exact moment. "And she's psychic. This is her calling now."

"Happy first day of work, chick!" Jazz screamed when I clicked over.

"Thank you. I was just talking to Isis. She's stopping for coffee, thank God. She might be an even better coworker than at my last job," I teased.

"Don't play with me. I was the best coworker you've ever had, and no one will ever take my place. Now how's the new house? You and Junior make a baby yet?" she asked. "I've been trying to give you some alone time and not call so much because y'all still in the honeymoon phase. Catch me up."

"The house is great, and no, we haven't since the last time we talked two days ago." I sighed. "But we are practicing."

"I bet. How's the racing team going? Has he hired any fine drivers or mechanics yet? Are they single?" Jazz asked.

"Not that I know of. Right now it's just him and Lo Jack. That's about it," I told her.

"Lo Jack? Oh God, I'm gonna need him to get some better employees. Why him of all people?" Jazz's response was reminiscent of mine when I found out Junior had invited Lo Jack, a shade tree mechanic and part-time criminal, to be a part of his new venture in Houston.

"Because not only is he one of the best mechanics around, but according to Junior, he's a hell of a driver," I explained, leaving out the fact that the latter was proven by his being the getaway driver for several robberies. As crazy as it sounded, it did make a lot of sense.

"I guess," Jazz said.

"Thanks for calling and cheering me on for my first day, bestie. I will miss working with you," I told her.

"Me too. But Isis will be a great fill-in until you come back home." Jazz sighed.

"What makes you think I'm coming back home? We love it here so far." I gasped.

"You haven't even been there a month. We'll see. But who knows? Maybe if you continue to love it, I'll move out there."

"Start packing your bags. Isis and I will be waiting for you with open arms," I bragged. "I'll call you later."

The call ended just as I turned into the parking lot of the clinic and pulled my car into the spot designated for me. A few of the other staff members arriving at the same time gave me pleasant smiles as I got out of the car. It was such a beautiful day that I almost regretted not allowing Junior to change my mind about coming to work. But I was looking forward to the day ahead and everything it had in store. My heart was full. Everything in my life was new: marriage, city, job, house, car, and it felt good to finally be at a place of peace. We'd survived chaos, fear, and danger, and now our lives were finally normal.

Chapter 3

Life was busy, but it was good. Because of the constant influx of patients, my days at the clinic went by extremely fast. I loved treating the women, many of whom were either expecting or new moms. It was fun seeing the excitement as they shared their ultrasound pictures or learned the sex of the baby, or when they would come in with photos of their new arrivals, and some even brought the newborns in with them. I was in heaven. The vibe in the office was positive, and most days I was surprised when it was time to leave.

"You got plans for the weekend?" Isis asked as we walked out of the office on Friday evening.

"Not anything in particular," I said. "We're still getting to know the city."

"You guys should go stargazing at Brazos Bend State Park. It's so romantic," Isis suggested. "Or you could go to the MoonStruck Drive-In and check out a movie. Again, so romantic."

"Have you been there?" I asked. Isis had been a great resource for whatever I needed in the city and as a lunch buddy. Much like her sister, she was a great listener and fun to talk to. She constantly had ideas and suggestions for places Junior and I could go or see, the best grocery stores, malls, restaurants, bars, everything. But she really didn't talk about her own life. I knew she had a longtime boyfriend, Tony, and had been waiting for him to propose, but it hadn't happened yet.

"Not recently. I mean, Tony and I go out, but nothing too adventurous." She sighed. "But you guys should really get out and enjoy the city."

"Hey, there's nothing wrong with some Netflix and chill. That's our favorite pastime. We do a lot of that."

"Okay, Netflix and chill is why you're gonna end up being our newest patient." Isis grinned. "I see that baby fever on your face every time someone brings a baby into the office."

"A little," I stated. "Junior has it way more than I do. If he had his way, I'd get pregnant today."

"Really? I thought you were ready to be a mom."

"I am, when the time is right. I think I just want to enjoy it being just the two of us and get a little more settled first."

Being a mother was something I was looking forward to. I knew Junior was going to be an amazing father, and he'd proven to be a great provider and protector. I just felt like we needed to wait a little while longer. I hadn't told him yet, but I figured as long as we were practicing making the baby, it wasn't a problem.

Isis and I said our goodbyes, and I headed home. My plan was to shower and change, then start the perfect romantic dinner. I'd taken some steaks out to be thawed by the time we got home for him to grill along with a couple of lobster tails and shrimp. They would be perfectly paired with my twice-baked potatoes, corn on the cob, and grilled asparagus. For dessert, I planned on making his favorite banana pudding. Dinner would be followed up with a candlelit bubble bath we'd share in our Jacuzzi tub and then whatever happened next. We both deserved a relaxing evening, and now that the security system had finally been fixed, we could enjoy some much-needed uninterrupted quality time.

"'Baby, you give good love.'" I sang my favorite Whitney Houston song at the top of my lungs as I stood in the shower. The hot water rejuvenated my body as it cascaded down my body, freshly scrubbed with jasmine and lavender soap. I was relaxed, happy, horny, and so engrossed in the moment that I didn't even realize I wasn't alone.

"Yes, you do."

The deep tone of Junior's whisper and his hand on my hip startled me, and I screamed.

"My bad, baby. I ain't mean to scare you," he said after I turned around and smacked his bare chest so hard that the water splashed on his face. I expected his eyes to meet mine, but they were focused lower.

Before I could scold him, his mouth covered mine and all was forgiven, and the shower lovemaking session commenced. By the time we finished, there were no thoughts of dinner, dessert, or anything else. We were too tired to do anything other than fall asleep in each other's arms.

I thought I was dreaming when I heard Junior's cell phone ringing in the middle of the night. When he didn't move at first, I thought he was still asleep and probably couldn't hear the phone over his snoring. But when it rang a second time, he reached over and grabbed it off the nightstand, stared at it for a second, then put it back down before snuggling against me under the covers.

"Who was that?"

It was his turn to be startled. His eyes opened, and he looked surprised that I was awake and staring at him. "Nobody important."

This wasn't the first late-night call he'd gotten. Usually, he was in the habit of turning his phone completely off before going to bed. But it seemed that he'd forgotten. I wasn't insecure at all and wasn't worried about whoever it was calling, but I was curious, so I pressed the issue.

"Obviously they are, because they called twice, and you turned your phone off. Don't lie to me, Junior," I said matter-of-factly.

He paused for a second before speaking. "I promise it wasn't anyone important. It was just business, that's all."

I leaned up from my pillow. "Business? At this time of night, Junior? What speed-racing track is open at three in the morning?"

"Not that kind of business." He shook his head.

"Junior . . ."

"I know, Sonya, but it's not my fault. I put the word out that I'm no longer working for the family, but not everyone knows, so they call," he explained. "That's not my life anymore, I promise."

"I know. I guess it's gonna take some time for everyone to get used to, so I'll extend you some grace. But you need to let folks know that's not what you do anymore and you don't handle that side of things. And your family is gonna need to start giving them another point of contact." I knew I sounded ridiculous. The drug game was an entity that had its own set of rules. It wasn't as if Junior could send a mass email or text telling his contacts that he quit. It was going to have to happen the same way everything else did—through word on the street.

"If it'll make you feel better, how about I get a new number? Will that work?" Junior offered.

"That's not necessary. I'm not worried. But you need to let them know that not only are you not working but you're also married."

Junior's eyes widened. "Okay, got it."

"And you need to tell them that your beautiful wife, whom you adore, doesn't play, and you would hate to answer when they call you at a disrespectful hour with some bullshit that you don't even handle anymore." I smiled innocently.

"Oh, I'll definitely let them know." Junior nodded.

"Good," I said as I laid my head on his chest.

The following day, while Junior was out running errands, I called Jazz while prepping the meal that didn't get cooked the night before. She was filling me in on all the gossip regarding my former coworkers, and I was taking it all in when Junior called.

"Hold on, this is Junior. He's at the store and probably about to buy something we don't need," I said.

"Let that man splurge and spend. You know what they say—it ain't tricking if you got it," Jazz yelled. "You're a Duncan now, boo. You can have whatever you like."

I ignored her and clicked over. "Hey, babe. Everything's almost ready for you to put on the grill. You on your way home?"

"Hey, you," he said. "Not at this moment. I'm actually running a little later than anticipated. Lo Jack and I got some things to take care of here at the garage."

"Oh, okay, that's fine. I'll just put it away in the fridge until you get here. It's no big deal."

"Thanks, baby. I shouldn't be too late. And I promise I'm gonna grill those steaks you're marinating to perfection as soon as I get home."

"Love you, Junior. See you when you get here."

"Love you too, Sonya. I'll set the alarm from my phone." He added, "Oh, and make sure you keep that sexy sundress on but don't have anything on underneath."

"Wait, how . . ." I glanced over my shoulder at the tiny camera hanging in one of the corners of the ceiling. "I told you about spying on me, Junior Duncan."

"I wasn't spying. I was making sure my wife was safe and watching her sexy ass cook in the process." He laughed before hanging up.

I turned to face the camera and seductively pulled the yellow maxi dress I was wearing down on one shoulder until it almost exposed my breast but didn't. My phone immediately rang again.

"You play too damn much," Junior said before I could even say hello.

"Bye, Junior. See you when you get home." I waved.

"Hello?"

I looked down and realized Jazz was still on the line. "Oh, my bad. I'm back."

"I was about to hang up. You know how you and Junior like to be all lovey-dovey on the phone, and I wasn't trying to be on hold," Jazz said.

"It wasn't even one of those conversations. He was just letting me know he'll be later than expected, that's all. Now where were we?" I said.

Jazz and I stayed on the phone another hour as I finished the dinner preparations. After our call, I poured myself a glass of wine, went into the den, tucked myself under a blanket, and watched the Hallmark channel. Before I knew it, I'd fallen asleep, and when I woke up, it was almost ten o'clock and Junior still hadn't made it home.

I called him twice, but he didn't answer. My emotions were a mixture of anger and concern. Not only did I not have any idea where he was or what he was doing, but I also had no one to call. Other than Lo Jack, Junior didn't know anyone in the area. There was no point calling his family back in New York. First, I didn't want to alert them, especially if it turned out that nothing serious was wrong. And then, they were hundreds of miles away, and really there was nothing they could do. Instead, I sent him a text telling him to call me ASAP, then went upstairs to our bedroom.

After pacing the floor for another hour, I decided to go to bed. That was also pointless because there was no way I could sleep. I tossed and turned for hours in between looking at my phone every fifteen minutes. Finally, I heard the security sensor alert.

I quickly pulled the app up and watched as Junior eased his truck into the garage and parked beside my car. He looked exhausted as he slowly walked to the door and entered the house. I closed the surveillance camera off my phone, then patiently waited for him to finally come into our room. It seemed to take him forever.

I hope his ass ain't down there looking for dinner, because I damn sure didn't cook.

When Junior finally made it upstairs, I was sitting and waiting in the darkness. As relieved as I was that he was safe and not lying in the hospital somewhere with no identification, I was livid that not only had he been out so late without letting me know but had ignored my calls and texts. This was out of character for him, and I was taken aback.

"You're up," he said, stopping in the doorway.

"You're alive." My voice was cold and emotionless and so was my face. "I wasn't too sure since I haven't heard from you in hours."

"My phone died. I know that's no excuse, but—"

"You're right, it's not," I responded. "There's a charger in your truck, and if that didn't work, Walmart is open twenty-four hours, and you could've stopped and grabbed one or borrowed someone's phone, I'm sure."

"I really didn't think about that, Sonya. I'm so sorry." He walked over to the bed and tried to touch me, but I pushed him away.

"Spare me the apology, Junior. I don't wanna hear it. You're not sorry. You're foul. That's what you are. Do you know how worried I was?" I yelled.

"I know, baby, and like I said, I just didn't think."
Junior shrugged.

"Like I said, you're alive. I'm going to bed." I rolled
my eyes and pulled the duvet over my body as I lay back
down.

"Sonya, just let me explain."

I was too mad to say anything else. Junior tried talking
to me a little while longer, and then he finally went into
the bathroom. By the time he got into bed, I was fast
asleep.

"Delivery for Mrs. Sonya Duncan," a scrawny delivery
guy announced as he walked up to the receptionist area
carrying two vases full of roses.

"Another one?" Denise, the receptionist, groaned.

Isis looked over at me and said, "Y'all must've had a
hell of a weekend. Did y'all go out?"

"No, actually, we stayed in," I told her, taking the vases
from Denise and carrying them into my office. It was
the third delivery I'd gotten. On top of my desk was the
Edible Arrangements basket and the cookie bouquet that
had been delivered earlier. One thing was certain, Junior
was determined to get my attention. Giving him the cold
shoulder all day on Sunday had served its purpose. This
morning, I'd even left for work without a kiss or an "I
love you." I picked up my desk phone and dialed his cell.

"Hey, baby," he answered before the first ring ended.

"Hi, Junior. I just called to thank you," I said, admiring
the yellow roses, which were my favorite. "For everything."

"You don't have to thank me, Sonya. You deserve each
and every gift and more. I fucked up the other night, and
I'm sorry. I just, I don't know . . . Me and Lo Jack went to
meet this guy on the other side of town and—"

"It's fine, Junior. I just need for you to let me know what's going on, that's all. I'm not saying you gotta check in every twenty minutes—"

"If that's what you want, Sonya, then—"

"I don't want that. But I do want to know if you're gonna be caught up and later than you told me you were gonna be, that's all. You're the main one stressing how you want me to be safe and our house fully protected. I want to know that my husband is safe, too." I sighed.

"I am safe, baby. But I get it. It won't happen again."

"Good. Now please tell me these flowers are the last thing that's gonna get delivered here today. You're making me look real spoiled in front of everyone. You know that, right?"

"I want them to know you're spoiled. As a matter of fact, I need the world to know. I should hire someone to come in there and serenade you so they'll really see how much I adore you." Junior laughed.

"Oh God, you better not," I told him.

"Well, will you at least let me take you to dinner tonight?"

"I was gonna finally cook those steaks."

"Nah, you ain't cooking nothing tonight. I'm taking you out on the town, woman. We're going on a date."

"I'd love for you to take me on a date, Junior Duncan." I sighed, my heart filled with as much joy and excitement as the day we were married. I couldn't stay mad at him for long. He was too good to me, and the love we shared was enough to conquer anything headed our way and any problems we faced.

Chapter 4

"Junior?" I murmured as I rolled over later that night. I reached my hand out to touch his body, which should've been next to me, but it wasn't there. My eyes fluttered open, and I rose, turning toward the bathroom. I listened close but didn't hear anything. Finally, I got out of bed, calling his name again, this time a little louder. "Junior?"

There was no answer. I checked, but he wasn't anywhere in the house. He was gone and hadn't said a word. I grabbed my phone, noting that it was after four in the morning before calling him. Just as the call connected, the familiar sensor chirped, and I listened to the sound of the garage door opening. Anger began to swell in my chest, and I pulled up the surveillance camera.

"What the hell?" I gasped at what was on the screen.

Junior had gotten out of his truck, but he wasn't alone. Lo Jack was with him. They were both covered in blood. The back door was open, and they were struggling to take something out. My mouth fell open as I realized it was a body and they were bringing it into my fucking house.

Within seconds, I threw on my robe and slippers and was downstairs by the time they came through the side entrance that led to the garage.

"What are you doing?" I screamed, catching them by surprise and causing them to nearly drop the man.

"Sonya, baby, he's been shot. We need you to help," Junior pleaded.

"Shot? You shot him?" I shrieked.

"No, someone else did. We saved him," Lo Jack panted.

At that same moment, a moan escaped from what I thought was a corpse, scaring the shit out of me. The man was alive, but barely. If the goal was to keep him alive, he needed to get to a doctor, and soon.

"I'll call 911," I said, panicking.

"Sonya, you can't do that." Junior glanced at me.

"What do you mean, Junior? He needs medical attention. Look at all the blood he's lost." I pointed out what should have been the obvious.

"I know. That's why we brought him here," Junior explained, now stopped and standing in the middle of the hallway while he talked. "You're the best medical attention he's gonna get."

"Me? Junior, I don't . . . I can't . . ." I stuttered. The man's head rolled from side to side, and his eyes rolled to the back of his head.

"You can, baby. You're his only hope or he's gonna die." Junior stared at me. "If we take him to the hospital, whoever did this is gonna finish the job."

"Or he'll end up in a prison hospital," Lo Jack added. "Either way, he'll definitely end up dead."

This can't be real. This has got to be a fucking nightmare. I stared in disbelief for a moment, trying not to panic. I was confused and had so many questions, but there wasn't time to even ask. The only thing that mattered was that if I didn't do something fast, the man was going to die in my new house.

"Take him into the downstairs guest room," I instructed, ignoring the thought of the mess we were about to cause in the bedroom I was in the process of decorating. "Hurry!"

Junior and Lo Jack didn't waste any time continuing down the hallway into the designated room. I was right behind them, turning on the light as they got the man to the bed. Once he was laid down, they moved back as I rushed over to see exactly where the man was injured and the severity of his situation.

"Junior, I need towels and plenty of them. And grab my stethoscope," I said as I ripped the guy's shirt open. "And get the big first-aid kit, not that it'll be much help."

"Okay." Junior ran out of the room.

"Lo Jack, help me get these clothes off so I can see where he's been shot," I commanded, then asked, "What's his name?"

When he didn't answer, I glanced over and saw that he was standing and staring. "Lo Jack, now!"

"Huh?"

"What's his fucking name?" I yelled. "And get your ass over here and help me!"

I felt bad for yelling. The shocked look on his face mirrored how I felt, but there wasn't time for either one of us to process what was happening. We had to act fast.

"Kareem," Lo Jack said as he quickly made his way to the opposite side of the bed and began to help. "His name's Kareem."

"Kareem? Can you hear me?" I leaned over and spoke softly.

His eyes opened for a moment, then closed. *At least he's responsive, even if it's slight. That's better than nothing.* We finally got his blood-soaked shirt off. I scanned his upper body and found that the source of some of the blood was a gaping hole in his shoulder and his side. I used the torn shirt and held it against the wounds in an effort to stop the bleeding as I looked for more wounds.

"Hold this," I told Lo Jack. "And help me lean him up."

Lo Jack proved himself a dutiful assistant, continuing to act as a tourniquet with one hand and using the other to help me pull Kareem forward so I could check his back. Sure enough, there were holes where the bullets had gone through, giving me a little relief that they weren't still in his body and would need to be removed.

"Towels, stethoscope, and first-aid kit." Junior returned with everything in hand.

"Good, here." I reached my hand out. "Give me a towel."

He handed me one of the thick, oversized towels that had never been used, and I used it as a makeshift bandage against the hole in the back of Kareem's shoulder before we laid him back down. The bloody shirt Lo Jack held was replaced with another towel. Junior helped continue undressing Kareem, and I found another flesh wound on his hip. I wrapped a smaller towel around it.

"How is he?" Junior asked as I used my stethoscope and checked Kareem's vitals.

I glanced up at him, resisting the urge to tell him that he wasn't as stable as he could be if he had adequate care. Instead, I said, "Alive. That's all I can tell you right now. But, Junior, he has three gunshot wounds, and he's lost a lot of blood. He needs stitches and fluids and meds. Right now, all he has is Egyptian cotton towels."

"He has more than that." Junior walked over. I didn't even realize my hand was shaking until he grabbed it. "He has you."

"I'm not a doctor, Junior." I shook my head.

"You worked in the ER for years before you changed to labor and delivery. And you told me plenty of stories about how you were the one to save patients' lives because the doctors were too busy, too tired, too distracted, or just didn't care about countless young black men who had been shot," Junior replied. "You can save him too. I know you can."

I thought about the patients I'd saved and the dire situation I now faced. "But I had access to hospital equipment and—"

"I know it ain't gonna be easy, but we gotta try," Junior said. "That's all I'm asking."

Looking down at Kareem, who was now unconscious, I still had no idea who he was or how he ended up with multiple gunshot wounds. I didn't know if Junior's faith in my ability to save him came from his love for me or another place of divine faith. But he was right. We had to try.

"What time is it?" I asked.

Junior looked at his watch. "Almost five."

"If he makes it another two hours, he may have a chance. I can't even promise that," I told him. "It's gonna take a whole lot of effort and a whole lot of prayer."

Junior looked over at Lo Jack still applying pressure to Kareem's shoulder, then back at me. "Whatever it takes."

"Well, it's definitely gonna take more than this." I raised an eyebrow and held up the first-aid kit. If Kareem did indeed make it, we were going to need some real medical supplies, and I was going to need help getting them.

"Hey, girl, I'm sorry to call you so early, but it's an emergency."

"Wha . . . what's wrong?" Isis sounded as if she'd just rolled over in bed, and I was sure my call interrupted a deep slumber. I'd tried to at least wait until the crack of dawn, but time was of the essence if I was going to make this happen.

"Isis, I need your help. It's a matter of life or death, literally."

"What is it? Are you okay? Do I need to come and get you? Junior ain't put his hands on you, did he?" Isis's voice was now alert and full of energy.

"Oh, my God, no!" I almost laughed. "Junior would never do that."

"I'm just saying, you never can tell with these jokers these days. Are you sure?" Isis asked again. "Never mind. I'm on my way."

"Isis, please, that's not what this is about. I'm fine, and no one put their hands on me, I swear, especially not Junior."

Junior, who was sitting in one of the kitchen chairs that he'd brought into the guest room after I convinced him to shower and change, frowned at me. I shook my head and gave him a reassuring smile.

"Listen to me. I need for you to go to the clinic for me and grab some supplies. But I need for you to get them without anyone knowing, so you gotta go now before anyone gets there," I told her, hoping she would comply without needing answers right away. She was my only hope for getting the basic items I knew were available and on hand in the clinic. One, she had a key to the building and all of the supply closets, and two, she was the only person I could trust. She'd never mentioned it in the lunchtime conversations that we'd had, but I was sure that Jazz had mentioned who Junior was and the nature of his family's business. And even if she didn't know, she was about to find out.

Isis paused for an extended moment, then finally said, "Uh, okay, what do you need me to get?"

I ran off the list of items I needed her to get, then said, "I'm gonna send Lo Jack to meet you and pick them up."

"Damn, are you sure you're not hurt, Sonya?" Isis asked.

"I'm not, but someone else is. I will explain later, I promise," I said, praying that she'd agree to do this.

"Okay, I'm getting dressed now. Give me thirty minutes, and I'll have everything you need." Isis sighed. "Tell Lo Jack to meet me at the gas station on the corner from the office."

"You are a lifesaver, literally," I gushed. "I appreciate this."

"No problem. I don't know what's going on, but I hope you're safe. If that dude has hurt you—"

"He hasn't, Isis, and he never will. I told you I'll tell you everything later. But I need you to get this to me as soon as possible," I reminded her. Then before she could say anything else, I told her, "Thanks again, girl. Bye."

"Did she think I hit you or something? Why would she think that?" Junior stood and asked.

"I don't know, Junior. Probably because I'm calling her at oh dark thirty in the morning, asking her to steal medical supplies with no explanation." I shrugged. "Trust me, I've never given her any other reason to assume anything like that."

I turned my attention back to Kareem. I'd somehow managed to stop the bleeding, but he needed stitches. For the third time, I used the home blood-pressure machine I'd luckily found in the linen closet, and I confirmed what I already knew: his blood pressure was extremely low.

"Lo Jack, I need you to go and meet Isis." I said, "Here's the address to the office, but don't go there. Go to the gas station on the corner. She'll meet you there. She drives a silver Maxima."

"Okay." Lo Jack, still wearing his blood-soaked clothes, jumped from his chair and nodded. "You need anything else while I'm out?"

"No, not unless you can get him something for the pain, because he's gonna need it." I sighed. There were a limited number of pain meds at the office, but not only were they kept under lock and key, but they were monitored very closely. Having Isis steal supplies was one thing, but stealing drugs wasn't something I wanted to risk.

"Oxy, morphine, or tramadol?" Lo Jack asked.

I raised an eyebrow, stunned by his question and the number of options. "Uh, I mean, we don't know if he's allergic to anything, but I guess whichever you can get."

"I can probably get all of them," he said. "How many do you need?"

"However many you can get." I glanced over at Junior, who shrugged as if we were discussing doughnut options for breakfast instead of prescription pain meds.

"A'ight, I got you. Kareem's a good dude, man. I hate that this happened to him." Lo Jack sighed.

"Be careful and keep your eyes open." Junior gave him the keys to his truck. "Call me if you see or hear any—"

"Junior, I got you. I'll be back within the hour," Lo Jack told us and walked out.

"Thank you, baby." Junior reached out and pulled me to his chest. "You were a lifesaver, literally."

"Don't thank me yet, Junior. He's still alive, but barely," I reminded him.

"That's better than dead," he replied just as his phone rang.

It was way too early for a business call, and his only employee had just left. I exhaled loudly, "Really?"

Junior looked at the phone and said, "It's O. He's calling about what happened. I gotta take it."

He was just about to answer when the alarm system blared.

"Shit, Lo Jack must've set it off." Junior groaned as he pulled up the app and tapped, silencing the loud noise. "Shit."

"What's wrong?" I asked, noticing the strange look on his face.

"Uh, nothing. Somebody's at the—"

The ringing doorbell finished his sentence, preventing him from doing so.

"Who the hell would be at our house, Junior?" I gasped.

"Don't worry, Sonya. I'll take care of it," he said before he rushed out. "Stay here."

My heart raced as I remained in place. I didn't know what to do. My mind was all over the place, and all I could think about was that whoever did this to Kareem might have come to finish the job or, worse, kill my husband. There was no way I was going to just stay back and let that happen. Without hesitating, I rushed out of the room and down the hallway. I arrived just as Junior opened the front door.

"Where is he? Where the hell is Kareem?" a woman standing in the doorway screamed.

Chapter 5

"Calm down," Junior told her.

"Calm down? What the fuck do you mean, calm down? My phone's been blowing up all night with people calling and texting me. They're saying he's dead! I called every fucking hospital in the city, called the damn morgue, and nobody don't know shit. The police found his car, and it's all shot the fuck up. Finally, I convince some broad at the cell phone company to give me his location, and it's this address." The woman was talking so fast that she was panting. "Where the fuck is he, Junior Duncan?"

The fact that she knew Junior's name caught me off guard. I remained near the hallway entrance, watching the exchange and waiting. She was an attractive woman, short and petite. Her cropped top, leggings, and fanny pack were typical attire for a twenty-something, as were her braids, which were just as colorful as her outfit. But the weathered skin of her face told me that either she'd lived a hard life, or she had to be in her early thirties, maybe both. One thing was certain, she was hardcore and wasn't afraid of Junior at all.

"I know you're worried, but—"

"No, bitch, you're the one who needs to be worried! I swear to fucking God, if you did this and then brought his body here to cover up your bullshit, I am gonna empty out." She held up the .40-caliber pistol that I hadn't noticed until that moment.

"Calm the fuck down, Keisha," Junior warned. "You know I'm the last person to be pulling a gun on."

"Stop telling me that!"

I wasn't as patient as my husband. I knew an irrational, emotionally distraught woman when I saw one, and I knew the repercussions. Why he was taking so long to tell her the obvious, I didn't know. This wasn't the time for chitchat or machismo.

"Kareem isn't dead. He's alive," I stepped up and said. Keisha looked from Junior to me, but she continued aiming the gun. "Now like he said, calm down and put that down."

"Who the fuck are you?"

"She's my wife and the woman who saved Kareem's life," Junior said, then in a swift motion grabbed the gun from her hand.

"He's alive?" Keisha frowned and tried to move past him, but Junior stopped her.

"Yeah, he is," he said. "And he's being taken care of."

"I wanna see him." Keisha growled the words through clenched teeth. Being disarmed by the person she was trying to gain entry from certainly didn't humble her.

"Nah." Junior shook his head. "That ain't happening."

"What the fuck do you mean, no?" Her voice went up two octaves. "Are you lying to me? Is he alive for real? Don't lie to me."

"I'm not lying to you, Keisha. He—"

Keisha leaned and looked past Junior's body. "Is he alive for real?"

I nodded. "He is. But he's unconscious."

For the first time since arriving on our doorstep, she softened. "Please, please let me see him."

"Keisha, you need to go." Junior reached for her, but she pulled away, still staring at me.

"I just want to see that he's okay," she continued pleading.

I looked at Junior and nodded slightly. "Yeah, you can see him."

He moved slightly so that she could pass, and I led her down the hallway to the room where Kareem lay unmoving. As soon as we walked in, Keisha gasped and ran to his side.

"Oh God, Kareem!" she cried. "All this blood . . . and his eyes aren't open."

"Like I said, he's unconscious," I explained. "We stopped the bleeding for now."

"For now? Then what? And why the hell isn't he in a hospital?" She turned and directed the question at Junior, who now stood in the doorway.

"You know that couldn't happen, Keisha. Kareem got warrants, and they would've immediately taken him into custody," Junior told her.

"So you just gonna let him lie here?" Keisha snapped and threw her arms up in disgust.

"Look, I know you'd prefer that your boyfriend was—"

"My boyfriend ain't got shit to do with this!" Her head turned so fast toward me that her Crayola braids smacked the side of her face.

"My bad, your husband?" I shrugged, looking back down at her hand in case I'd overlooked a ring, but there wasn't one.

"Ain't nobody got no fucking husband." Keisha rolled her eyes.

"I'm her . . . brother."

The voice was low and raspy and caused all of us to turn and look at where it came from.

"Kareem!" Keisha ran over to the bed and leaned over her brother. "You are alive."

I grabbed my stethoscope and the blood pressure cuff off the dresser and checked his vitals. "How are you feeling?"

"Like . . . shit," Kareem whispered, his eyes remaining closed.

"You should," Junior said. "They tried to take you out, man. You a soldier though."

"Soldier for who? Don't act like this was some act of heroism. We all know why he's lying here in this bed, Junior. You knew he shouldn't have been making that drop by himself. They hit y'all three times in the past two weeks," Keisha said.

"This ain't on me," Junior replied. "I—"

"Is there another fucking Duncan around here running shit?" Keisha snapped back.

Running shit? Why would she say that? The only thing Junior was running was his new racing company. He didn't have anything to do with anything that happened to Kareem. Keisha was wrong. At least, I hoped she was, for his sake.

"Kareem?" I called his name, but he didn't respond.

"What happened?" Keisha asked. "Kareem?"

"He's unconscious again," I told her. "He'll probably be in and out for a while."

"I can't believe this shit. It should've never even happened." She glared at Junior. "You know what's been happening around here, and you sent him out there anyway. He was a fucking target."

"You act like I—"

"How about both of you calm down?" I said, then turned to Junior. "Can you check on the supplies I ordered?"

"Yeah." He sighed and walked out.

I checked Kareem's wounds to check the bleeding. The towels covering them were still bloody, but they weren't soaked. That along with the fact that he'd momentarily gained consciousness were definite signs of improvement.

"Is he gonna be okay? It's so much blood," Keisha said.

"We stopped most of it, and once he's stitched up—"

"And when is that gonna happen? If you had taken him to the ER, they woulda at least stitched him up," she shot back at me.

I pursed my lips and reminded myself that this situation had everyone stressed and everyone should be extended a little grace, including this disrespectful-ass woman whose brother I was trying my best to save.

"I agree, but he was brought here, so I'm doing the best I can right now," I told her.

"Lo Jack is on his way back now," Junior walked in and announced.

"Good," I said. "I'm gonna go and take a shower and change. And I need to call the office and let them know I won't make it in this morning."

"Go ahead, baby. I'll keep watch." Junior kissed my cheek.

"Let me know if anything changes, and if he wakes up again, make sure he doesn't move. We don't want the bleeding to start again," I stated.

Keisha stared at me as I walked past. As soon as I walked out the door, I overheard her talking. "Damn, I thought folks was joking when they told me you got married."

"Well, it wasn't a joke. And as you can see, my wife is not only beautiful, but she's a straight angel on earth. You need to keep that in the forefront of your mind," Junior told her.

"I respect it. I guess I'm just surprised. You used to always tell me that commitment wasn't your thing."

"It wasn't, until I met the right woman," he replied.

"I guess." Keisha sighed. "If my brother dies, it's on your hands, not hers."

"He's not gonna die. Sonya knows what she's doing."

"And what the fuck is it that you're gonna do, Junie?"

I frowned at the name Junie. Something about the way she said it made me uneasy. Certainly, it wasn't a nickname I'd heard anyone else use before. The strange familiarity I sensed before between the two of them was now even more unusual to me.

"Lower your damn voice, Keisha. What do you mean? I was the only one who went to his rescue, and I brought him here so he wouldn't die." I could tell that Junior was straining to talk low, but I could still hear what he was saying.

"I'm talking about the fact that Kareem was on the fucking clock when this happened. He was working for your family. Now what the hell are y'all gonna do about it? Ain't no way y'all are gonna let whoever did this get away with it. This wasn't about my brother. This was about business, and you know it. Now it needs to be handled."

I tensed, now piecing together what transpired and why Junior felt so compelled to bring this man to our home. I should've known that it had something to do with the underworld of the Duncan family. Keisha was mistaken though. This wasn't on Junior. He was no longer associated with that side of the business, and therefore, he wasn't about to get involved.

"I already made a call to Orlando, Keisha. No one's gonna get away with this, I promise," Junior answered. "We know how valuable Kareem is not just to you, but us. He's owed that much."

"I appreciate that," Keisha said softly. "You're a good dude, Junie. Always have been, and I am thankful that you had Kareem's back and you went to help. We all go way back. Kareem is the only family I have."

"I know, Keisha. He's gonna pull through this."

"You promise?" Keisha's loud sniffles let me know that she was crying.

"I promise," Junior told her. "And I promise I'm gonna make this right for you and him."

It got quiet for a moment, and I listened closer as I stood a few feet away from the doorway. *What the hell?* Just as I was about to go back into the room, Junior walked into the hallway. We both jumped, surprised to see one another.

"Oh."

He said, "I thought you were upstairs, baby."

"I came down to make some coffee before I showered," I lied.

"I can make that for you."

"No, I'm good. I need you to do something else for me."

"Anything. Just tell me." He gave me a loving look, and I almost changed my mind about what I was about to say.

"I want you to tell me what the hell is going on, and I mean *everything*, Junior Duncan." I looked him directly in the eye.

"I'm trying to piece it together now. Kareem was on his way to do a drop, and—"

"I'm not talking about that, Junior. Or should I call you Junie? What the hell is up with you and Keisha?" I demanded, not concerned about the volume or tone of my voice, unlike him.

Junior stared at me for a moment, but he didn't say anything.

"And don't lie to me," I added in case his delayed response happened to be caused by his attempt at thinking of any response other than the truth.

"There's nothing going on with me and Keisha," Junior said, then mumbled, "Not anymore."

My eyes widened, and I stared at him in disbelief before turning around and rushing up the stairs into our bedroom. I didn't bother closing the door because, the entire time, I heard Junior's footsteps behind mine as he called my name. I paced back and forth, hoping that it would help calm the anger that was growing inside of me by the second. Bringing an injured man into our house was one thing, but this was something else. *Ain't no damn way. This is too much.*

"Sonya, I told you I'd never lie to you, and I didn't." Junior had enough sense to give me six feet as he talked to me.

I stopped pacing long enough to give him a death stare. "Is that supposed to make me feel better? Because it doesn't." I resumed adding to the step count for the day, shaking my head in disgust.

"No, that's not what I'm trying to do," Junior said. I glanced at him again, and he realized his error and tried to clean it up. "I mean, there's no need for you to even be worried about Keisha at all. That's what I'm trying to say. I dealt with her a long time ago, and I mean long."

"I can't tell, not the way she's strolling up in here acting like she's in charge and reminding you of how much y'all mean to each other." I reminded him of the conversation I'd overheard in case he forgot.

"You got it all wrong. Kareem has worked for us for years."

"Who the hell is us, Junior?" I threw the question at him.

"He's worked for my family. This whole situation is complicated right now, but I promise it's gonna get taken care of. O is sending the twins and DJ down here right now."

"So now you're going back to your old job?"

"No, not at all. Look, that's not on me. Orlando is taking care of that part of the situation. The only thing you and I have to be concerned with is getting Kareem fixed up enough so that he can get out of here and go home. That's it. All that other stuff is irrelevant, including Keisha,"

Junior told me. "I'm sorry she showed up like this, and I apologize for not going into detail as soon as she got here, but I tried to stop her from coming in."

"So now this is my fault?"

"No, it's not. It's nobody's fault, Sonya. It is what it is. She's Kareem's sister. We used to deal with each other a while ago, but it wasn't serious at all. And I damn sure ain't marry her. I married you. You are the only woman I fell in love with, which is why I am willing to do anything to make you happy."

As he stared at me, my heart melted from the love in his voice and his eyes. I didn't say anything, but he must've sensed that it was okay for him to come closer, because within seconds, he was gathering me into his strong arms and kissing me as if he needed me to feel everything he'd just said. I allowed myself to be caught up in the moment, enjoying the taste of his mouth as it covered mine. The truth of the matter was that I couldn't stay mad at Junior for long. I had a past the same way he did. At least he'd been honest about Keisha. When my ex-husband made his presence known, Junior had been blindsided because I had never mentioned him. But he forgave me, and we got through it together. Now we would do the same thing.

Chapter 6

By the time I was showered and changed, Lo Jack had returned with everything I'd requested. He seemed just as uneasy and surprised to see Keisha as Junior had been. I walked downstairs and found him talking to Junior in the hallway.

"Man, I thought that was her I saw when I left, but I thought I was tripping. I can't believe you let her in here. You know she's trouble. This ain't good, Junior."

"It's cool. Sonya said it was okay, and I already checked her," Junior told him.

"Yeah, but Sonya don't know that y'all used to—"

"Sonya does know, Lo Jack," I said as I walked up. "Junior told me everything."

"He did?" Lo Jack gave me a surprised look.

"I did. I don't lie to my wife or keep secrets." Junior pulled me to his side.

"That's what's up then," Lo Jack said, obviously impressed by our united front. "Well, I got everything from Isis. That's one sexy-ass woman, I swear. She still ain't single, huh?"

"No, she isn't." I shook my head. "And don't you have enough baby mama drama to worry about anyway?"

"That's why I need a good woman by my side like you. The three of them be tripping," Lo Jack said. "I put the box of supplies in the room. Oh, and Isis said to tell you she talked to your boss and everything's cool."

"Thanks. Dr. Whitman told me when I called that she'd explained I had a family emergency," I told him.

"You need me to do anything else?" he offered.

"No, you've helped out enough for now," I said. "Go home, shower, and get some rest. Thanks again, Lo Jack."

"No problem."

"Uh, I'ma need you a little later. Be on standby," Junior told him. The look they exchanged didn't go unnoticed.

"Always, boss." Lo Jack nodded. "I'll take your truck to the garage and make sure it's cleaned up. Then I'll get someone to bring it back here."

"Nah, not here. My house is off-limits to everybody at this point. Just pick me up after it's done," Junior told him.

"Let me get in here and get started," I said, taking a deep breath before walking in the room. *It was a long time ago. It was a long time ago,* I repeated in my head. To my surprise, Keisha was gone. "Junior?"

"Yeah?" Junior rushed inside.

"Where's Keisha?" I asked.

"She left. I told her it was pointless for her to hang around and I would keep her updated. Besides, she and Lo Jack don't get along, and I didn't need them going back and forth anyway."

"Good."

"Oh, Sonya, I almost forgot." Lo Jack popped into the room and held out a paper bag. "Here you go."

I took it and looked inside. I couldn't believe the contents. "Wait, how did you—"

"Don't worry about all that. Like I said, Kareem's a good dude. His sister, on the other hand, is a bitch, and I can't stand her, but this dude is solid. I made a couple of calls and got what you needed. Let me know if that'll work." Lo Jack shrugged.

"I think this will definitely be enough." I looked back at the mini pharmacy in the bag. Not only had Lo Jack somehow gotten the pills I requested, but there were a few vials of Propofol.

"A'ight, I'm out," Lo Jack said.

"How the hell did he—"

"Baby, I ain't ask because I don't even know or care to know. I've learned the street game is just like the military. There is a 'don't ask, don't tell' policy in place." Junior laughed. "You sure you gonna be able to handle this by yourself?"

"I'm sure, baby." I nodded.

"Okay, I got some calls to make. I'll be right in the den if you need me." He kissed me, then looked at Kareem. "You're gonna be a'ight, man."

When he was gone, I went through the supply box Lo Jack had placed on one of the chairs, then arranged everything on the dresser the same way it would've been in the ER. Surprisingly, there wasn't much that I didn't have. Isis might not have known exactly what was going on, but she clearly had an idea because she'd pretty much provided me with a makeshift operating room. I slipped a pair of surgical gloves on, said a quick prayer, then went to work as if I were in one of the finest hospitals in the city.

After injecting a small dose of pain medicine into Kareem's arm, I carefully washed his wounds on the front of his body, then sutured and dressed them. Once they were finished, I called for Junior, who came in and helped me turn Kareem over so I could do the same for the exit wound on his shoulder.

We spent most of the day and night taking turns watching him. By nightfall, his vitals had improved, but he was still unconscious.

"I wish we could change the linen," I said when I checked his bandages. "He needs clean linen. Maybe that will help."

"Baby, he's fine. You performed surgery on him in a four-thousand-dollar bed," Junior pointed out, then suggested, "He's probably too comfortable to wake up."

"True, but these bloody sheets are irritating me and they're not sanitary." I sighed. "Maybe we can shift him in the bed and change them. Go get another set out of the closet please." I batted my eyelashes.

"First you were complaining about me bringing him here to save, and now you giving him VIP treatment." Junior laughed. "I'll be back."

"Thank you," I heard. I looked down at Kareem staring at me.

"Oh, you're welcome. How are you feeling?"

"Like I've been in a drive-by shooting." He gave me a half-smile. For the first time since he arrived, I noticed how handsome he was.

"As you should," I told him, placing the stethoscope on his chest. "I gave you a little something for the pain. I can give you more."

"Nah, pain is a sign that I'm still alive." He groaned as he tried to sit up.

"Don't do that," I scolded. "Those are sutures in your arm, not staples. We don't want them to rupture. You gotta take it easy."

He relaxed back on the pillow behind his head. "Yeah, I might need a little something."

"I got you." I nodded.

"You a doctor?"

"A nurse, but I've been in enough hospitals to know what I'm doing. Don't worry." I looked through the pain meds and decided which one to give him.

"Oh, shit, you're awake." Junior walked in, carrying the sheets.

"No shit, Sherlock," Kareem told him.

"Is that any way to talk to the man who saved your damn life?" Junior grinned.

"I think that compliment goes to that lovely woman over there." Kareem nodded in my direction. "What's your name, Nurse?"

"Sonya. I'll get you some water so you can take these."

I returned with the water and helped Kareem sit up so he could swallow the pills.

"Thanks. You really married to this fool?" he asked.

"I am." I nodded.

"Damn, why? I mean, how the hell did he manage to convince you to do that? Are you here against your will? Blink twice. You ain't gotta say nothing." Kareem laughed as he closed his eyes. Moments later, he was asleep. Junior and I retreated into the den.

"He's out for the night, you think?" Junior frowned.

"Probably. Lo Jack scored some pretty powerful stuff," I told him.

Junior's phone chimed. "Speaking of Lo Jack, he's here to get me. You gonna be okay for a couple hours? I gotta go meet up with DJ and the twins too."

"Yeah, that's fine. But, Junior, I meant what I said."

"I'm not gonna be involved, Sonya. I just have to make sure they know what's up, that's all. This ain't on me," Junior insisted. "Orlando got it under control. This is his job now."

"I'll be here when you get back," I told him. After he was gone, I curled up on the sofa and called Isis to thank her for her help.

"I'm just glad everything is okay," she told me. "You coming in tomorrow?"

"No, I'll probably be out a couple more days. I talked to Dr. Whitman, and he understood. I feel bad about taking off so soon. It couldn't be helped though." I sighed.

"So this family emergency, is the person okay?" Isis asked. I knew she was waiting for the details, but I wasn't ready to share them just yet. We were cool, but not that cool. If anything, I had to tell Jazz first before telling anyone.

"Yeah, they're fine," I said. The sound of the doorbell caused me to sit up.

"Is that your doorbell?" Isis asked.

"Girl, yeah. Hold on one sec." I pulled up the security app. My eyes widened at the sight of Keisha standing on the front landing. "Isis, lemme call you right back."

"You sure? I can stay on the phone in case you need me."

I knew she was trying to be nosy, and as much as the thought of her being within earshot made me feel a little better, I declined. "Girl, it's Uber Eats. I'm fine."

"Uh-uh, girl. You need to click the button where they just leave your food on the doorstep. It's dangerous out here."

"I'll remember that next time," I said. "Call you tomorrow."

When the call ended, I pulled the app up again and spoke into it. "Can I help you?"

The camera had a clear shot of Keisha as she jumped for a second, then looked around. Had I not been so put off by her showing up on my doorstep, I would've been amused.

"It's Keisha!" she looked at the camera and yelled.

"Okay, can I help you?" I repeated my original question.

"Uh, yeah, you can come open the door. I wanna see my brother." Keisha spoke as if I couldn't comprehend English.

"He's resting. Junior told me he was updating you." I sighed.

"I'm not here for no updates. I wanna see my brother." Keisha looked frustrated. "Now let me in."

"That's not happening," I told her.

I watched her reaction. It was a mixture of both surprise and frustration, much like the way I reacted when I saw her on the screen of my phone.

"I don't have time for this shit. Where the hell is Junior? Tell him to come and open this fucking door right now before I—"

"Keisha, what the fuck are you doing at my house? You need to leave right now!" Junior's voice came from nowhere. He had to have been using the app.

"You come and open this door, Junior Duncan!" Keisha screamed.

All I could think about was how we'd barely moved into the high-class neighborhood and this ghetto chick was causing a scene at our front door. The last thing I wanted was the neighbors to see or hear anything, especially since we hadn't met any of them yet.

"Keisha," I said in the calmest voice I could muster, "Kareem is asleep, and he will be for a while. He took pain meds about an hour ago. There's nothing you can really do for him right now but stare at him while he's asleep, and I'm sure you got way better things to do tonight. Come back tomorrow, and I promise you can see him."

This wasn't the first time I'd had to have this conversation. Working in hospitals had prepared me well, and I had plenty of experience. I prayed that Keisha's dumb ass would have enough sense to accept what I'd said and leave. I'd been polite, but I could get real disrespectful if I needed to.

"This is some bullshit, for real," she mumbled.

I watched her for a second until finally she turned around. Just as she was about to walk away, Junior issued a final warning.

"Oh, and your ass better call before you come, too, Keisha."

Keisha looked back at the camera and angrily raised her middle finger before stomping off. I watched the screen until she got into the Dodge Charger sitting in front of my house and sped down the street.

I wasn't surprised to see my wedding photo flashing on the caller ID on my cell phone as soon as I closed the security app. I was tired and had enough drama for the night, and I thought about ignoring the call, but instead I answered.

"I'm sorry about—"

"Junior, please stop apologizing. I don't want to hear another 'I'm sorry.' It ain't helping this crazy situation at all." I exhaled into the receiver.

"I know, but I feel bad that you even have to deal with all of this. It's just . . . I didn't plan on—"

"Look, I know you didn't plan for any of this happening. It's not like you shot him. You were just trying to save your friend, and you did. And I'm glad I was able to do that," I told him. "But what I'm not gonna allow is for anyone to come in and disrespect me or our house."

"You won't have to. I'll make sure Keisha understands that."

"I'm trying, Junior, because I know she's worried about her brother, and with good cause, but I'm not above cussing her out either."

"You ain't gonna have to do that, I hope, but if you feel the need, I don't have a problem with it." He laughed. "I knew you were a gangsta when I married you."

"You have no idea." I sighed. "I'm gonna check on Kareem, then go lie down for a while."

"I'll be home in an hour or so."

I was sure Junior believed that he'd be home within that time span. And I wanted to believe him. But with everything that had transpired over the past few days, I wasn't sure, nor did it matter. I had more important things to concern myself with, including making sure Kareem remained stable. The quicker he healed up, the quicker he could leave our home and this entire ordeal would be over.

Chapter 7

I spent most of the night checking on Kareem every three hours while trying to nap in between. Each time, I was relieved that he seemed to have improved a little, but he was still in serious condition. As I suspected, Junior didn't return home until almost three in the morning. I'd just returned to my bed after doing my routine check on Kareem when I heard him easing into our bedroom. I listened as he took a quick shower, and before long, he was nestled beside me, snoring loudly. I smiled as I drifted to sleep.

A few hours later, I slipped from the weight of his arm and returned to my nursing duties.

"Good morning, Sonya."

A small shriek escaped from my throat as I walked into the bedroom. I hadn't expected anyone other than Kareem to be there. Instead, DJ, a longtime member of Duncan security, was leaned back in the chair.

"DJ, what the hell?" I hissed.

"My bad. I ain't mean to scare you." He smiled and sat up.

"What are you doing here? When did you get here?"

"We got here early this morning."

"We?" I asked.

"Yeah, Carl and Carlos are out front. Junior told me to stay in here and watch him." DJ motioned toward Kareem. "He's been asleep most of the time though."

"Most?" I raised an eyebrow.

"Yeah, he woke up once and looked at me. Asked who the fuck I was, and I told him. Then he went back to sleep."

I pulled a pair of gloves on and tended to Kareem instead of marching upstairs and waking Junior up to ask why he felt the need to have security at our house. It dawned on me that whoever had done this to Kareem may have found out he was here. That meant that none of us were safe.

"I'll be right back," I told DJ, rushing out of the room and back upstairs. "Junior!"

"Huh?" Junior's eyes opened and he looked around for a moment.

"Junior, get up." I pushed his shoulder.

He sat up and looked at me. "What's wrong, baby? Is it Kareem? Is he worse?"

"No, Junior, Kareem is fine. DJ is down there with him." I tilted my head.

"Oh, okay. You good?" Junior gave me a concerned look. "You sound upset."

"I am upset. I know you said DJ and the twins were coming, but I didn't know they were coming here. And why are they here? Is there something else going on that you aren't telling me about? Obviously so, if half the Duncan Security detail is here." I tried to hide my frustration, but I no longer could. "Is someone after you, or us?"

Memories of our running from my ex and his gang members came flooding back to me. We'd had to hide and look over our shoulders at every turn, damn near living like prisoners in our homes. It had gotten so bad at one point that Junior ran away from his own family in an effort to keep them safe. I hated living in fear, and now that Charles was behind bars and his gang had been uprooted, I thought all of that was behind us.

"What? It's nothing like that. I brought them here to look out for dumb-ass Keisha in case she popped up unannounced, and I figured DJ could help look out for Kareem so you wouldn't have to do it by yourself," Junior explained.

"You're lying," I said. "I thought Orlando sent them to clean up the mess caused by whoever ambushed Kareem."

The look on Junior's face let me know that I was right. "I mean, yeah, there's that, too."

"Why can't you just be honest, Junior?" I threw my hands up in disgust.

"I am being honest. They're here to keep watch, but just until Kareem is strong enough to move somewhere else."

"Somewhere else like where?" I asked.

"I haven't figured that part out yet, either a hotel or Airbnb, somewhere safe. I heard you last night when you said you weren't going to be disrespected. I don't want Keisha back in here. The sooner we get him out, the less we see of her," Junior told me. "They're here more for him than anyone."

"You think whoever did this knows that he's here?" I asked.

"No one other than Keisha. And she knows if she tells anyone, it puts her brother back in danger, and she ain't gonna do that. The safest place for him is here, but he damn sure can't stay here."

"Hey, Sonya," DJ called up the stairs. "He's awake."

"I have a patient to go check on."

When I got back downstairs, Kareem was more alert than he had been since Junior and Lo Jack dragged his body in through the garage. I smiled at him. "Good morning."

"Mornin'"

"You look better."

"I still feel like shit, but that's better than dead." He grinned, then told DJ, "This lady is my angel."

"Yeah, Sonya is like that. We all love her. That's why her ex ain't wanna let her go." DJ grinned. I shot him a threatening look, and he quickly said, "I mean, she's a real one."

"Speaking of letting go . . ." Kareem looked over at me. "A brother gotta use the bathroom."

"That's a good sign," I said. "DJ, can you help me get him to the bathroom?"

DJ jumped up, and we aided Kareem out of the bed and onto his feet. From his grimaced face and slight moans he made with each step, he was still in a lot of pain, and there was still a little drainage from his shoulder wounds. It took some time, but we finally made it to the bathroom and got him to the toilet.

"You ain't really gotta stay in here." Kareem glanced over at me as I stood in the doorway.

"You sure? I'm a nurse, and I've already seen all of you, remember."

"I know, but can a brother hold on to at least a little dignity?"

"Fine, I understand." I closed the door so he could have some privacy. A few minutes later, I tapped on the door. "Ready?"

There was no response, so I tapped again.

DJ, standing a few feet away, looked at me. "You think he's a'ight?"

"I don't know, but we need to check." I opened the door and gasped. Kareem was slumped over and passed out. "DJ!"

DJ rushed in, and in one swoop, he lifted Kareem up and rushed him back into the room. My plans to finally change the sheets were a bust now. We got him back on the bed.

"Kareem." I rubbed his arm.

"Should I call Junior?" DJ panicked.

"And what is he gonna do?" I asked. "What you can do is hand me that pencil light off the dresser."

DJ grabbed the light and looked over my shoulder as I used it to check Kareem's pupils. "He still alive, right?"

"Yes, DJ. He's just passed out." I sighed, relieved that Kareem hadn't gone into shock. "He moved too fast and too soon. His pressure dropped a little. It'll come back up, I hope."

"Guess he shoulda used a bedpan," DJ suggested. I made a mental note to have Isis grab one of those for me when I talked to her.

"What's going on?" Junior walked in.

"Kareem just had a slight relapse when we took him to the bathroom," I told him.

"A relapse? Damn, that ain't good."

"He's fine though. I'm sure he'll wake up in a little while."

"Any chance of that happening anytime soon?"

"I don't know. Why?" I frowned.

"Because I just told Keisha she could come and see him." Junior's face had the same regret that I felt when he said it.

"How long you gonna keep him on these dirty-ass sheets?" Keisha sucked her teeth as she pulled one of the empty chairs beside the bed. Kareem was still unconscious, but his blood pressure was back to normal.

"Until he's stable enough for me to change them," I told her. "His condition right now is too fragile, and we need to keep him as still as possible."

"He was awake earlier though and talking," DJ offered. I noticed the way he and the twins were checking Keisha out when she arrived. Her tight jeans and shirt tied at the waist left little to their imagination.

"He was? And no one called me so I could talk to him? See, this is what I'm talking about. I told—" she started but was stopped by the twins running up on her.

"Seems like you forgot the instructions you were given before you came in," Carl told her.

"You raise your voice or cause any problems, we're hauling your ass outta here," Carlos added.

Keisha looked him up and down and looked like she wanted to say something, but she didn't. I didn't know if it was because she was afraid or from the sheer shock of how quickly they seemed to appear out of nowhere. Either way, her demeanor swiftly changed, and she became polite.

"You got forty-five minutes left of your one-hour visit." Carl tapped his watch and gave her a warning look.

"Can I at least get the Wi-Fi password?" She glanced over at me. I stared back without saying a word until she finally sighed and said, "Please."

"It's 'Duncan4life.' The number four, not the word." I exhaled.

"Thank you." She gave me a smile that I knew was fake. I really didn't care, especially since she would be out of my house within the hour. "I'll leave you to your time. DJ, I'll be upstairs."

"Wait, he's staying in here with me?" Keisha frowned.

"He is staying in here with your brother," I told her. "You can leave if that's a problem, of course."

"Nah, it's whatever. I'll be glad when he can get the fuck up outta here," she mumbled under her breath.

"You and me both," I said loud enough for her to hear as I walked out of the room. One of the things I hated most while working in the hospital was when doctors rushed patients being released before they were well enough, but at this point I was tempted.

God must've heard the prayers of both Keisha and me, because by the time she returned for her one-hour visit the next day, Kareem was alert and talking. He still wasn't able to get out of bed, but with the help of DJ, I was able to roll him over and finally change the linen and give him a sponge bath. After sitting up, he looked ten times better, and I could see that he was well on his way to recovering.

"Reem, you're up!" Keisha smiled.

"Yeah, I am." He didn't look too thrilled to see her. "What's up?"

"What do you mean? I'm here to check on you." She turned her nose up.

"I guess I'm just surprised, that's all. You know how you don't really be that concerned these days, and you know why." Kareem shrugged.

"Don't be like that, Reem. You're the one who's been actin' funny, not me. But either way, I'm here and I'm glad you're better. Now we can get you outta here and back to your own crib where I don't need permission to see you." Keisha cut her eyes at me.

"Well, I ain't in that much of a rush considering the fact that the care I been getting is beyond sufficient, and I'm grateful to be here," Kareem told her.

"I heard that." Junior walked in and gave Kareem a light dap.

"I'm serious, man. That's real talk. Thank you."

"It's all love, man. You know how we do." Junior nodded. "And you know this ain't going away quietly."

"I ain't got no worries about that either." Kareem gave a nod of his head.

"Funny, because when I brought that up, you were acting like you ain't wanna have nothing to do with that," Keisha commented. "Now, all of a sudden, you got his back."

"I never said that." Junior frowned.

"And I know better than that. You being messy, Keisha, and I know why." Kareem cut his eyes at her. "You're in your feelings."

"I ain't being nothing. I don't have no need to be in my feelings. Think what you want, but my man makes sure I'm good, and I do the same for him. Junie ain't the only one who got a real one," Keisha bragged.

"A real fool, that's what your man got. And if Dynamo really had you, you wouldn't be doing what you're doing for him," Kareem responded.

"Dynamo?" A surprised look came across Junior's face. "You're kidding, right?"

"I wish," Kareem answered.

"You're tripping. Don't act like I ain't always been ride or die. You both know better than that, including you."

The fact that her last comment was directed at Junior didn't go unnoticed. I was too engrossed in the conversation to care and didn't want to interrupt.

"True, but Junior ain't never have you pushing weight or in harm's way. That damn sure ain't making sure you're good. That's getting your dumb ass to do his dirty work, and you're so desperate that you do whatever he says." Kareem shook his head. "It's embarrassing."

"Says the man who's been transporting shit for the past twelve years for the same 'friend' and ain't moved up the ranks yet. Who's the fool?" Keisha jumped up. "You know what? I ain't gotta stay here and listen to this shit. You're right. I am a fool. A fool for even driving way the fuck over here to check on your ass. I'm outta here. And don't worry. I won't be back."

We all watched her as she stormed out of the room, and a few moments later, the sound of the front door slammed, letting us know that she was in fact gone.

"Her dumb ass don't even realize she doing me a favor." Kareem laughed. "She's my sister, but she's trouble. Always has been."

"I can't believe she's fucking with Dynamo. That dude is the worst." Junior shook his head.

"I hate to ask, but who's Dynamo?" I finally asked.

"A local knucklehead turned two-bit hustler who thinks he's a kingpin but ain't got enough sense to even understand how the game is run. That's why he latched on to Keisha's dumb ass, because she's smart and she knows shit," Kareem explained. "She's right. She's always been ride or die, but she's gonna end up getting killed if she ain't careful. She's playing a dangerous game."

"Hey, man, what she said about working for—"

"Ain't nobody thinking about what her dumb ass said. We both know what it is, and it's been that way since day one. I ain't got no complaints, Junior," Kareem told him. "Except for the fact that a nigga is hungry as hell."

"Well, if your nurse says it's okay, we can get DJ to get you some food. Hell, I think all of us are hungry right now." Junior laughed.

"What you say, Doc?" Kareem looked over at me. "Can a brother eat something?"

"Of course he can. But how about I cook instead?" I offered.

Kareem smiled. "She cooks, too? My dumb-ass sister ain't never stand a chance. Shit, I may never leave."

Chapter 8

I was finally able to go back to work on Thursday. Kareem was stable enough to be moved to what Junior referred to as a "safe house" and would be accompanied by DJ, who would stay with him for a few more days. I'd offered to come to wherever he was moved to change his bandages and check on him, but Junior assured me that he'd found someone to take over once he was moved. For me it was bittersweet. As dramatic and unexpected as this situation had been, I really liked Kareem and, in a way, didn't want him to go.

"Are you sure whoever you have checking on him knows what they're doing? Are they even licensed? I mean, he's better, but his injuries—"

"Baby, he's going to be fine. We hired a professional licensed home health aide." Junior sighed.

I'd stopped in to do one final check on Kareem before leaving for work, even though I'd already done so a few minutes before. "Home health aide? You didn't get him a nurse, Junior? And you could've at least let me check this person out."

"Doc, we all know that whoever it is ain't gonna be as good as you. But I promise you I'm gonna be okay." Kareem grabbed my hand, then turned to Junior. "Well, as long as whoever he hired is fine, I will be."

"What you think, DJ?" Junior asked.

"I mean, I don't really look at guys like that, but your new nurse Henry isn't a bad-looking guy." DJ shrugged.

"What?" Kareem yelled, causing all of us to laugh.

"For real though, Doc, I'm good. And when I'm back on my feet, I'ma be over here for some of that macaroni and cheese you made."

"And I'll make it for you." I leaned over and kissed his cheek.

"Ooh-wee, Junior, and she smells good, too. Man, you better hold on to her, because if I ever get the chance to get close to her, I'm taking her."

Junior snatched my hand away from him. "That ain't never gonna happen, fool. Baby, aren't you gonna be late for work?"

"Oh, now you worried about me being late? A few minutes ago you were telling me I shouldn't even go." I touched the side of his face. "But you're right. I'll call and check on you in a little while, both of you."

"Best doc in the world," I heard him say as I walked out.

"Best wife in the world," Junior corrected him.

"Best cook in the world," DJ added.

I had just pulled out of the driveway with a satisfied smile when my phone rang. I answered without looking, expecting it to be Jazz calling for an update on the situation. I'd been filling her in daily, making sure she understood that she wasn't to share this with anyone else, including Isis.

"Hey, girl," I sang into the speakerphone.

"Well, hey, girl, to you too," a voice that didn't belong to Jazz replied.

I stuttered. "Mrs. . . . uh, Chippy, I thought you were someone else. Good morning."

Chippy Duncan was my mother-in-law. Our relationship was a little rocky at first, for good reason, but we'd gotten a lot closer since the wedding. She wasn't too thrilled about our decision to move across the country and start a new life, but she was definitely supportive. We would text a few times during the week, and we talked weekly, mainly on Sundays. Until she called, it didn't dawn on me that we hadn't talked. We'd had so much going on, I hadn't thought about it.

"How are you, darling?" Her voice was warm and soothing and made me miss her.

"I'm good. How are you?"

"Missing you and my son, of course. But I'm glad to know that you're holding up, especially under the circumstances."

"Yeah, the move has been a lot, but you know I started my new job, and we're getting settled in our house." I laughed nervously.

"And having to take care of a gunshot victim in your guest bedroom probably was a bit stressful, I'm sure."

I was so stunned that I almost missed my turn to get on the interstate. Her knowing about what was going on shouldn't have come as a surprise. The Duncans were a tight-knit family. Keeping their secrets from the outside world was one thing, but keeping them from one another wasn't something they normally did. There was no telling how she'd found out. Even if she hadn't heard about it directly from Junior, once anyone in his family became aware, then it became shared knowledge among the Duncan clan.

"It was a little hectic at first, but we took care of it," I said.

"I heard *you* took care of it. And I'm glad. I know the past few days haven't been easy, but you've done well, and I'm proud of you. You're a Duncan for sure." Chippy laughed.

"Thank you, Chippy. I appreciate that."

"Before long, you'll be the new Mrs. Brewer for the family."

Mrs. Brewer was the go-to medic who took care of not only the Duncans, but anyone associated with them who couldn't be taken to the regular hospital, much like Kareem. I understood why Junior felt comfortable bringing him home to me.

"I'm definitely not trying to earn that title," I quickly spoke up.

We said our goodbyes, and a few minutes later, I arrived at the office. My nerves were a little shaky as I entered the building. Isis had assured me that no one even noticed the missing supplies she'd gotten for me, and no one asked any unusual questions about my being absent.

"Welcome back," the office administrator greeted me. "We missed you."

"We did." Isis turned and nodded.

"I missed you guys too, and I'm glad to be back," I told them, then continued down the hallway to my office.

"Girl, I wasn't expecting you to come in today. I thought you'd be out all week," Isis said as she walked in behind me.

I made sure the door was closed behind her. "Why would you think that?"

Her question made me a bit nervous. Jazz promised that she wouldn't mention to Isis any details about what happened, but the two were close. Although I trusted my best friend with my life, there was always a slight possibility that she'd slipped up. If there was a chance that Isis knew anything, she would have to be the one to reveal it, and I damn sure wasn't going to confirm it.

"Because if I missed Monday, Tuesday, and Wednesday, ain't no way I'm coming in Thursday and definitely not Friday. This place wouldn't see me until Monday morning." Isis laughed.

"I get you, but I didn't want to miss the staff meeting. It's bad enough I missed three days this week," I explained and relaxed a little, telling myself that I was being paranoid. "Dr. Whitman has been gracious about me being absent, and I want to show him that the practice is still a priority."

"I guess." Isis sounded as if she still didn't understand my explanation, then said, "But I'm glad you're back. I'm glad things are better."

"Much better. Thanks for all of your help, too. I appreciate you."

"We're family, girl. That's what we do. Lord knows you're the only person I'd put up with Lo Jack's nonsense for." She laughed. "I gotta admit he is kinda cute though. But I already know he's trouble."

"And you would be right." Although he'd proven himself quite useful, there was no way I was going to let Isis even consider dating Lo Jack.

For the past few days, he'd been a member of what had become the Kareem Crew at my house. Junior and the guys, including Lo Jack, DJ, and the twins, would gather in the guest bedroom and, according to Junior, shoot the shit until the wee hours of the morning. Sometimes their laughing and talking would be so loud that it would drift all the way upstairs into our bedroom, where I spent most of my time. But there would also be serious, hushed conversations and deep murmuring that would quickly hush whenever I walked in the room. Something about those alerted me that although Junior said he wasn't involved with the street side of things, he was still connected to it. His brother Orlando was scheduled to arrive later in the day, which hopefully meant that he would take charge of whatever needed to be done, and not my husband.

"I got enough trouble with the man I got. I don't need any more." Isis sighed.

"How about you tell me all about it during lunch, my treat?" I offered. "It's the least I can do considering you had my back this week. I know I had you doing some crazy stuff."

"You don't have to do that, Sonya. It wasn't that crazy, although the bedpan request threw me for a loop." Isis shrugged. "I ain't gonna turn down a free meal though."

"Great," I told her. "Now get out so I can at least get a little work done before the meeting."

I shooed her out of my office and sat down, trying to get myself together before the staff meeting. I wanted to call and check on Kareem, but Junior assured me that if anything went wrong or he needed me, he'd call. *Get it together, Sonya. Everything's gonna be fine. Kareem is on the mend and being moved someplace safe. Now life can go back to normal.* Closing my eyes, I took a few deep breaths.

"Sonya?" There was a soft tapping at my office door.

"Yeah?" I called out. "Come in."

Dr. Whitman stuck his head in. "I'd like to speak to you before the meeting. You got a moment?"

"Sure," I said with a nervous smile, wondering if Isis had been wrong and he had noticed the supplies missing or, even worse, he was concerned about my absence and wanted to address me face-to-face.

"I'm glad you're back, especially today, because I have some concerns that I'm going to address with the staff about security and protocol."

"Security and protocol?" I repeated. My heart was pounding.

"Yes. As much as I enjoy our being a part of this community, there are some safety concerns." He sighed. "The other day, there was a robbery and shooting nearby at Dr. Yung's dental practice. And that building was just as secure as this one. I'm hoping that isn't going to be anything that we have to deal with, but I'm not willing to take any chances."

"I understand." I nodded, then half listened as he talked about possibly hiring a security guard for the office and a few other items he wanted my opinion about. It was funny, because I thought leaving New York and moving to Texas would be safer for Junior and me, but now that wasn't happening at all.

Once the staff meeting was over, my morning was busy with nonstop patients. I didn't even have a chance to think about Kareem. It wasn't until Isis and I were at lunch and Junior called that I remembered. I excused myself from the table and went outside to take the call.

"Hey, baby, how's your day?" Junior asked when I answered my cell.

"It's pretty busy, but good," I told him. "How's Kareem? Was he in a lot of pain during the move? Did you make sure to grab his meds so he'll have them?"

"We haven't moved him yet. But I will make sure he has them."

"What? I thought you were taking care of that first thing this morning."

"Something came up. The twins and I are headed to the airport to pick up O, and we'll get him moved and settled right after that. And before you ask, DJ is there with him. He's fine."

"Okay." I sighed. "Well, I guess I'll see you when I get home. I probably will stop at the mall before I get there. A sister needs a little retail therapy."

"Take all the time and therapy you need, sweetie. You deserve it."

"I deserve something else, too, a whole lot of it. We haven't had any alone time in a few days," I reminded him.

"Oh, don't worry, you're gonna get plenty of that, too. I plan on making up for lost time." The lustful tone of his voice caused the heat to rise in me. There was nothing sexier than knowing he was looking forward to pleasuring me as much as I was planning to please him. I was horny, and now that this ordeal was coming to an end, I was gonna make sure we spent plenty of time together in bed, in the shower, on the sink, hell, anywhere the mood hit us.

"I can't wait." I giggled. "Maybe I'll buy something to wear for you later."

"Don't bother buying that. You won't have it on long enough for me to even see it, I promise." He laughed.

"I love you, Junior Duncan."

"I love you, Sonya Duncan." He hung up.

Damn, I didn't even tell him about his mother calling me. That man has me so gone that I can't even think straight.

"Everything okay?" Isis asked when I got back to the table.

"Yeah, everything is fine." I nodded as I sat across from her.

"I bet." She chuckled. "Junior must've whispered some real good nothings in your ear."

"Why you say that? And how did you know it was him?"

"Because of the way you floated back in here and that wide-ass grin on your face."

"Fine, it was him. And he said for me to go shopping after work. You wanna come or nah, nosy?" I asked.

"Wait, free lunch and we hitting the mall after work, too?" Isis gasped. "Oh, Jazz is really about to be mad because you're about to be my bestie. I'm taking you from her."

Chapter 9

It was well after dark by the time I made it home. I tried calling Junior, but he didn't answer. I suspected it was because he was busy with Orlando and making sure Kareem was moved and settled. His unavailability was a win for Isis, because we went to dinner at one of the restaurants that she'd been suggesting. After pulling into the garage, I grabbed as many of the shopping bags that I'd accumulated during my mall outing with Isis as I could. Once inside the house, I went straight to the bedroom. Instead of hanging my purchases up, I set the bags into the closet. The next stop was the bathroom, where I filled the tub with water and some of my favorite bath oils. Remembering the candles that I'd bought earlier, I headed back to the closet before starting to undress. As I passed the window facing the rear of the house, I heard something.

"What the hell?" I peeked out the curtain and looked closer, but I didn't see anything. Just as I was about to close it, I saw something flashing for a brief moment, and then it was dark. "What in the world?"

I grabbed my phone off the bed and pulled up the security app just in time to see a shadowy figure moving toward the house, and then the screen went dark. I tapped the screen again, but it wouldn't pull anything up. I exited the app and tried to restart it, but it wouldn't. The system wasn't working. I heard a noise coming from downstairs. Someone was in my house. I slowly eased toward the doorway and listened.

"You sure this is the house?" a man asked.

"Fuck yeah, I'm sure. This is the address," another voice answered.

"I don't even see how he is still alive. We filled that fucking truck full of holes."

They were looking for Kareem. They'd come to finish the job. *Thank God he's gone. Hopefully they'll see that and leave.*

"Shit, that nigga ain't here now, but he was. Look at these bandages and shit," the first man said. "For all we know, he just might be dead after all. Come on, let's go."

Good, they're leaving.

"Hold up, man. Let's not be too fast. I mean, if this is Junior Duncan's crib, that nigga gotta have a safe or some money stashed somewhere," the second voice told him.

"Shit, you right," his partner responded.

I knew that their search wouldn't be in vain, and they wouldn't leave until they found something for their trouble. I had to do something and do it fast. After turning off the light, I tiptoed to the closet as fast and as quietly as I could toward the only thing I had to protect myself. My hands fumbled in the darkness as I reached in the far corner of the shelf, praying hard as I touched the metal case.

"God, please help me," I whispered, snatching it down. My fingers trembled as I put in the code that Junior insisted I memorize "just in case." I carefully removed the handgun and hid as far back in the closet as possible. With my eyes closed, I waited and tried to remain as calm as possible, taking slow, deep breaths.

You can handle this, Sonya. Whatever it takes to survive, you can and will do it. You are a Duncan, and Duncans are always ready for war.

"In here!" I heard a voice enter the bedroom. "Yo, hold up. Someone's here. There's water in the tub!"

"Shit, it must be his girl. They said she wouldn't be home!"

I held my breath and knew I had to make a decision. The next place they'd be headed was toward the closet. I had to get them before they got me. I stood slowly with the gun aimed toward the door.

"She gotta be in the closet!"

I began counting backward, my finger positioned on the trigger. "Five, four, three, two . . ."

Pow! Pow! Pow!

I screamed and fell to the floor, crawling back to the far corner, still clinging to the gun that I had yet to fire. My entire body was shaking, and I feared for my life as the closet door, now riddled with bullets, opened. A tall shadow stood in the doorway.

"Sonya, you good?"

I opened my eyes and cried out, "Kareem?"

"Yeah."

I scrambled to my feet and scurried out. "Oh, my God."

On the floor beside him were two bodies, both bleeding onto the hand-knotted wool and silk rug. I didn't bother checking the pulse of either as I stepped over them and grabbed hold of Kareem, who was holding his shoulder.

"You sure . . . you good?" Kareem panted.

"I'm fine," I said, putting my arm around him and helping him out of the room. "Slow, easy, I got you."

He leaned on me, trying to move as fast as his body would let him, grimacing with each step. By the time we made it back downstairs and into the guest room, we were both drenched in sweat. My first instinct was to check him to make sure he was okay, but I had another major concern.

"We need to get out of here now!" I said. "There may be someone else with them."

Kareem shook his head. "No, it was just them two, and I'm pretty sure they're dead. But we need to call Junior!"

"My phone is upstairs." I tossed my hands up and shook my head. "And how do you know it's just the two of them? And where the hell is DJ? You weren't even supposed to be here."

"I know. Something went down, and he got called away. I got a feeling that all of this shit was a setup, Sonya. We've gotta call Junior," Kareem said, reaching into a duffle bag that held his belongings.

"You don't think anything's happened to him, do you?" I asked, realizing how dumb I must've sounded considering Kareem hadn't left the house and had no way of knowing.

"I damn sure hope he is okay," Kareem said, dialing a number then putting it on speakerphone.

I waited for what seemed like an eternity, praying that Junior would pick up. Instead, his voicemail answered. "Damn it, Junior. Where the fuck are you?"

"Lemme see if Lo Jack answers. They're probably together."

Before he could dial, we heard the garage door opening. Kareem grabbed his gun and went to sit up. He looked over at me and said, "Get in the closet."

"No," I told him and held up the gun I was still holding. "I ain't going nowhere."

I positioned myself near the door while Kareem remained in bed, but we both remained armed and ready for whoever was about to enter.

"What the hell? The damn security system ain't working. Sonya! Baby, you here?"

Kareem and I gave each other a confused look.

"Junior?" I yelled out. "I'm in here."

"Yeah, baby." Junior came charging into the room. He grabbed me and pulled me into his arms, then looked at Kareem. "You hear what happened to Lo?"

Kareem frowned. "Nah, but wait 'til you hear what happened to us."

"What you mean? What happened?" Junior looked at me.

"Someone broke into our house, Junior. They were looking for Kareem," I told him.

"What? Stop fucking playing!" Junior released me. "Who the fuck was it? Where are they?"

"Their bodies are upstairs on our bedroom floor, baby," I told him. "Kareem shot them."

"This is crazy. Someone let shots off at Lo Jack's baby mama's house earlier." Junior began rubbing his temple. "That's why we needed DJ!"

"Oh, my God, is she okay? Is he?" I gasped.

"Everyone's fine so far." Junior sighed. "This is crazy. I need to call Orlando. We gotta find out who the fuck is doing this shit."

"I know who it is," Kareem said.

Junior and I both looked at him and spoke at the same time. "Who?"

"That fucking Dynamo."

"What? Why would you think it was him?" Junior asked.

"I recognized one of them dudes as one of the young boys he's got working for him. It's gotta be him."

"I'm calling Orlando," Junior said, then told Kareem, "You know what to do."

"I'll go ahead and put the word out right now." Kareem nodded and looked down at his phone.

Junior took me by the hand, and we stepped outside the room. I lowered my voice. "What the hell, Junior? All of this . . . this is too much . . . I don't—"

"I know, Sonya."

"No, you don't know," I said through clenched teeth. "There are two dead men—well, I think they're dead—upstairs."

"Which is why I'm gonna need for you to leave for the night," Junior told me.

"What? And where the hell am I supposed to go?"

"You can go back to the suite at the hotel." He put his hands on the side of my face and looked me in the eye. I looked past the worry and saw the love, but it didn't help the fear that was building in my chest.

"And what about you, Junior? And what about Kareem? We can't leave him here by himself." I pointed back to the door of the guest room.

"I'll handle that. But I need to make sure that you're safe first and foremost."

"He's right, Doc. You're his priority and rightly so," Kareem called out. "Listen to Junior. He'll look out for me, but he can't do that until he knows that you are good. He's got both of us. But you need to get out of here."

Junior pulled me toward the staircase. "Sonya, please, come on."

The last place I wanted to go was back upstairs, but I didn't have a choice. Everything I needed was in our bedroom: my purse, phone, and clothes. I had no choice but to allow Junior to lead me. When we got to the doorway, he looked back at me.

"You gonna be okay, baby?" His voice was full of concern.

"Junior, I'm a nurse. I've seen cadavers before. Not necessarily in the middle of my bedroom floor, but I've seen plenty of them." I nodded.

As soon as we stepped into the room, Junior turned on the light. Despite my levity moments before, the sight of the two dead men caused the hairs on my neck to stand. They were so young. I hadn't realized I'd stopped and was staring until I heard Junior call my name.

"Sonya."

"Huh?" I looked up at him.

"I'll grab your bag from the closet for you."

"Okay." I nodded. "I'll get my toiletries together."

I went into the bathroom and leaned against the marble sink, taking a moment to catch my breath. The water that I'd drawn was still in the tub, but now the bubbles were gone, and it was cold. All I wanted was to come home, take a bubble bath, and relax before making love to my husband. Why the fuck were we dealing with all of this? We were supposed to be making a baby. Now I was wondering if we even needed to be planning for one.

"You okay, baby?" Junior tapped on the door.

"Yeah." I jumped up and grabbed various items off the sink without much thought. The last thing I was concerned with was whether or not I had mouthwash.

Junior had my overnight bag and my suitcase on the bed waiting. He'd also covered the bodies. Although I was appreciative that he'd made an effort, the fact that he used the duvet from our bed to do so bothered me.

"Yeah, O, she's packing up to leave right now. To the hotel. Yeah. Okay," Junior said into his phone, then hung up.

"What about your bags?" I asked.

"I'll pack up later, let's get you out of here."

I tossed whatever items I could into the bags and zipped them up. Junior picked them up and ushered me out. I tried not to, but I couldn't help taking one final glance at the covered bodies.

"Don't worry, they won't be here when you come home," Junior assured me. "I'll make sure everything is as good as new, I promise."

"It's okay, Junior. I'm not worried about that," I told him. "I'm more concerned with all of us staying alive."

"I got that too."

As we headed back downstairs, his phone chimed. He looked at it and told me, "Uh, baby, I'll take your luggage to your car and pull it out front for you."

"Okay, lemme just check on Kareem before I go." I nodded.

"You getting outta here, Doc?" Kareem asked when I entered the room.

"Yeah, I just wanna make sure you're good," I told him. "Let me check that shoulder of yours."

"It's fine. I'm fine. Now you need to leave so you'll be fine."

"Kareem, if I need to leave in order to be safe, then so do you and Junior."

Kareem shook his head. "Nah, you need to be safe from witnessing the aftermath. Me and Junior ain't the ones in danger."

"Thank you for saving me." I kissed his cheek.

"Reciprocity, Doc. You saved me first." He smiled.

"Baby, you ready?" Junior called out.

"Yeah."

When I got to the foyer, DJ was standing beside Junior, who was handing him my keys. I stopped and frowned. My husband must've known what I was thinking, because he began explaining before I said a word.

"It's just until I get to the hotel, that's it."

"I don't like any of this, Junior Duncan." I exhaled loudly. "This is the shit we moved away from."

"You're right, and like I said, this is just temporary. Now you need to go." Junior kissed me, then held me in his arms a little longer than usual.

God, please watch over him. Keep him safe. I love him and don't know what I'd do without him. I closed my eyes and started praying that nothing would happen to him. I'd never told him, but part of the reason I was so willing to move was so that I wouldn't have to worry about his safety like I had when we were in New York and living with his family. Now it seemed like no matter where we went, we would still be targeted.

"She's gonna be okay, Junior."

My eyes fluttered open, and I stared at Orlando, who'd just entered the room. "Hey, O."

"Hey, sis." He walked over and hugged me.

"It's good seeing you. Wish it were under better circumstances, but it's still good to see you." He smiled.

"It's good seeing you too, Orlando." I nodded.

Orlando glanced over at Junior, then back to me. "Listen, once we've finished handling these business meetings, we'll definitely take some time to sit and catch up before I head back to the city. DJ?"

DJ gave Junior a look and said, "I got her."

"Y'all need to head out," Orlando told him.

I reluctantly allowed DJ to escort me out the front door to my car. He opened the door, and just as I was about to get in, a car pulled up and parked in front of the house. I paused for a second, waiting to see who it could be. My eyes widened when Keisha stepped out and raced toward the door.

"What is she doing here?" I spoke aloud.

As if she sensed me questioning her presence, she paused and stared at me. "Where's Junior? And how the hell did he let this happen to my brother? He was supposed to protect him. Now he's gone."

"What?" I asked, confused.

"Sonya, get in the car. We gotta go." DJ gently nudged me. I looked over at him, and he shook his head. "Get in."

I followed his instructions and got into the car without saying another word. He closed the door and ignored

Keisha, who continued yelling toward us. Within seconds, both Junior and Orlando were walking out the door toward her. The last thing I saw as we drove off was them damn near carrying her inside.

"DJ, what the hell was she screaming about?" I asked. "Why does she think something happened to Kareem?"

"Because word on the street is whoever tried to take him out the first time finished the job." DJ shrugged.

"What? Word on the street?" I frowned, then remembered Kareem telling Junior he'd make a call and put the word out. "Wait, so you think Keisha had something to do with all of this?"

"Who else knew where Kareem's been this entire time?" DJ answered. "Or it could be one helluva coincidence. Either way, you play stupid games, you win stupid prizes. And the last people you wanna play with are the Duncans."

Hours later, Junior arrived at the hotel suite. Instead of pretending to be asleep, I jumped out of bed as soon as I heard him come inside. He'd barely walked through the door before my arms were around his neck. The tears I'd held on to for what seemed like days erupted and flowed down my face.

"It's okay, baby, it's okay. I'm fine, Kareem's fine, you're fine, everyone's fine. It's over. I promise it's over," he whispered as he rubbed my back.

My uncontrollable sobs prevented me from speaking, so I just nodded my head. He held me close until I was finished. When I finally lifted my head, he used his fingertips to brush away my tears, then kissed me. It seemed like an eternity since we'd shared a deep, long, passionate kiss. I didn't want it to end—not the kiss or the moment.

I quickly began to unbutton his shirt and pulled it over his head. The surprised look in Junior's eyes turned to desire, and he slipped the straps of my satin gown from my shoulders and nibbled along my neck. It didn't take long for us to undress as we made our way farther into the suite, but we didn't make it to the bedroom. Instead, we stopped in the living area, where he laid me back on the sofa and proceeded to devour my wet center like a wandering man in the desert who'd just discovered a lake. I begged him to stop, but he refused, tasting me until my satisfaction was evident by me climaxing over and over again.

Just when I thought I couldn't take it anymore, he turned me over and entered me from behind. It wasn't the tender lovemaking that we typically enjoyed. My husband was fucking me, and I enjoyed every moment of it. The pent-up frustration that we both had been holding on to for the past few days released, and by the time we finished, we were sweaty, exhausted, and breathless.

"Damn, Sonya, you are one helluva woman. Everyone tells me I married the right woman, but they have no idea." He held me in his arms. The sofa was much smaller than the king-size bed in the next room, but there was no way I was going to move.

"Funny, they tell me that I married the right man."

"Guess we're perfect for each other, huh?" He laughed.

"We are. And we make one helluva team, too." I sighed.

"We definitely do that," he agreed. "I love you, and you know I wouldn't do anything to put you in harm's way, right? You have to know that."

"I do." I closed my eyes.

"And I mean it when I say that the nightmare we've been living the past week is over. Dynamo is taken care of and done. We don't have to worry about any more bullshit," he murmured and rubbed my shoulder before kissing it.

I didn't have to ask what he meant. I already knew. I waited a few seconds, then raised my head up and looked at him. "Junior?"

"Yeah, babe?" he whispered.

"What about Keisha?"

He opened his eyes and looked at me. "Like her brother said, smart girl, but she picked the wrong team. Play stupid games, win stupid prizes."

Chapter 10

A week later, I stood outside of our home watching Charlene as she hammered the FOR SALE sign into the grass. It was a bittersweet moment, but I was relieved. As much as I loved our first home, there was no way I was ever going to sleep there again. Junior was right when he said everything would be cleaned up and good as new. The bodies were gone, the carpet replaced, and the closet repaired within a day. But one thing he couldn't remove or fix was the memory of what had taken place in our bedroom. We had to go.

"Welp, that's the last of it." Junior pointed to the two guys carrying the final items from the house toward the large moving truck in the driveway.

"Okay." I sighed. "I guess that's it."

"Mr. and Mrs. Duncan, I'm sorry this home wasn't up to par for you. I really thought this would be the perfect starter home for you and suit all your needs," Charlene told us. "But don't worry, I have plenty of other options for you all to check out, or we can always design a home, and you can have it built to your specifications. Whatever works for you."

Junior smiled and put his arm around me. "You know, Charlene, we appreciate the offer, but I think we're gonna hold off on that."

"Are you sure?" She frowned. "You're not leaving the area, are you?"

"We're positive. And no, I think we're just gonna enjoy five-star hotel living for a while. It seems to work better for us." I glanced up at Junior, and we laughed.

Girl Like Me

by

Kamaryn Hunt

Based on the song title
"Girl Like Me" by Jazmine Sullivan

Prologue

I need some dick. No, wait, I don't. I mean, I do, but it's not really a need. So really, maybe I should say I want some dick. Good dick. No, great dick. Great sex. Wait, that's not the case either. Well, kinda, but it's more than that. I want great sex with foreplay and afterglow. The kind of sex that's hot, nasty, and gratifying. Sex that leaves me satiated, depleted, and exhausted. Yet it also makes me feel connected, fulfilled, and certain. I want to feel close, be touched, kissed, cuddled, and fucked. Is that too much to ask?

I closed my journal and placed it back into the nightstand beside my bed, making sure it was pushed all the way to the back so no one would find it. I didn't know who that could possibly be, considering the fact that I lived alone. But in case some random burglar broke in and went rambling in my nightstand in search of hidden jewels or a stash of cash that wasn't there, my journal wouldn't be within their reach. My deepest thoughts would be safe.

One of my biggest fears was that something would happen to me and my family would have to come to my apartment for my belongings. I couldn't bear the thought of my semi-holy mother reading anything I'd written in the thick leather-bound notebook that, ironically, had been a Christmas gift from her. I say semi-holy because much as she loved God, gospel music, and the Bible, loved to cuss. Profanity was definitely her love language, and she enjoyed using it often. If she were to ever get a glimpse inside the pages, the level of judgment and colorful vocabulary that would accompany it would be of epic proportion. Lord knows I loved her, and we were close, but some things I just didn't need her to know. Like the fact that I really needed—correction, wanted—some dick.

Instead of spending any more of my limited time worrying about the safety of my journal, I got up, quickly made my bed, then proceeded to get ready for work. One thing my mother didn't have to cuss about was me being gainfully employed. I was self-sufficient and financially stable. I'd done everything "the right way," the way she raised me. Stayed out of trouble most of my life, graduated with honors from high school and finished cum laude from Texas Southern. I was immediately hired as a health administrator at one of the finest women's clinics in Houston, which thankfully saved me from having to go back home and live with her in San Antonio. I was doing well for myself, and she was proud. Hell, I was proud of myself. I had a nice car, a gorgeous place, and a decent job. Life was decent, and for the most part, I had nothing to complain about, which was why the fact that I still woke up daily feeling like something was missing bothered me so much. I was tripping.

"Get it together, chick," I said as I tossed a pair of scrubs on my freshly made bed, then headed into the bathroom.

Thirty minutes later, I was showered and dressed, and my braids were bonnet free as I walked out the door of my second-floor condo. I paused, looking over the railing at my neighbor tonguing down some woman in front of my car parked in front of the building. I waited thirty seconds, hoping their make-out fest would be over by the time I got to the bottom of the stairs, but they were still going at it. I had no choice but to pretend that they weren't there. I hit the unlock button when I was a few feet away.

"Oh, damn, my bad," he mumbled when the chirp of my alarm interrupted them.

"Excuse me." I gave them a dry smile as I opened my door and tossed my gym bag and purse into the passenger side.

"She's rude." The tall, statuesque, pretty woman whose skirt barely covered her ass glared at me.

I stared back, unconcerned about her or how she felt, especially since the chances of her ever seeing me again were slim to none. Moses "Moe" Kramer and I had been neighbors for over a year. I'd learned early on that there were three things he had plenty of: friends, parties, and women. He was a typical frat boy: good-looking, dressed well, made money, and liked to be the center of attention. I wasn't impressed, which was probably why we didn't care for each other.

"Let me walk you to your car. I gotta get ready for work." Moe put his arm around her, and they moved farther along the sidewalk toward the visitor spaces.

I hit the start button and was about to reverse when my best friend Karima called for the second time. I'd missed her first call while I was in the shower, and I figured she'd call back so we could enjoy our morning chat while we both drove to work.

"What up, what up?" I answered through my Bluetooth speaker.

"Heffa, I know you saw that I called you."

"I did, but I was in the shower," I explained.

"Then why you ain't call me back?"

"Because you called me before I got a chance to. I was gonna, but some thot had curbside checkout at Moe-tel Tricks this morning in front of my car." I sighed.

Karima laughed. "Not another one."

"Of course, this one was tall, nice weave, slim with a BBL," I said, describing Moe's latest conquest.

"At least he has a type." Karima giggled.

"Don't all of them these days? Pretty, petite, and pro-portioned—that's all a woman has to be for a man to be interested."

"That's not true. If that's the case, why are you and I single?"

"You're single because you want to be," I responded. "You definitely fit the basics that I listed. Hell, you're beautiful and bold, and your body is the bomb."

"And so are you," Karima quickly replied.

I knew that was what she was going to tell me. And deep down, she probably meant it. But Karima was five foot five and had never been bigger than a size ten. She had the same cute cheerleader shape she had in high school, only now her hips were a little wider and her breasts fuller. Everywhere we went, she'd turn heads.

"I'm not having this conversation with you this morn-ing. I'm already pissed that I'm not gonna have time to get Starbucks," I told her. "Now I'm gonna have an attitude until lunch. You know I need my coffee."

"You don't need Starbucks. Drink some green tea when you get to the office, and you'll be fine," Karim suggested, then continued, "You are beautiful and you know it, and before you say it, your body is fine. Hell, I wish I had some of that ass you got."

I appreciated my bestie being nice, and she was right, I did have a nice ass. But I also had a thick waist to go with it and chunky thighs. Men wanted the derriere but weren't too fond of the additional thickness I carried with it. Not the men I wanted, at least.

"You can have it," I said. "I'd gladly donate fat to the Karima Booty Improvement Drive."

"You are crazy. And there's no need for either one of us to do that. We've been hitting this gym, and we'll continue our routine until we both reach our goals. We putting in work, right?" she asked.

"Right." I sighed.

"And I have no doubt the universe will be sending both of us exactly the man we desire."

"Even though the man I—"

"Aht aht, nope. Now that's the conversation we're not having this morning," Karima said, interrupting me with a warning. "Now positive vibes, positive thoughts, and positive outcome all day long. You wit' me?"

"I'm wit' you," I relented and agreed.

"I'll see you at the gym at five thirty. And don't stop at Starbucks on the way there either," she said, issuing another warning.

"Not even to grab a water? You know Starbucks has the best water in the world," I whined.

"I'll have water waiting for you," Karima said. Then before hanging up, she added, "Leave the past where it belongs, Sierra—behind you. What you are seeking is seeking you. You just gotta make sure you're focusing on what's ahead, not dwelling on insignificant situations."

Karima had a tendency to exude spirituality in the mornings, which often resulted in her being a bit nuanced. It was a bit aggravating, but she meant well. I'd been trying to focus on the future, but it was easier said than done, especially since the "insignificant situation" happened to be a man who was now in my past but I presently desired daily. It was more than dwelling. It was a craving, much worse than the one I had for Starbucks. He was a skinny mocha latte with an extra shot of dark espresso of a different kind, and I wanted him bad.

Chapter 1

I was five minutes late when I pulled into the back parking lot of the clinic. I opted to enter through the side door, which led directly into the hallway where my office was located, hoping no one would notice. I loved my job, but a couple of my coworkers were a bit intrusive, and I preferred to stay to myself, at least in the mornings while I got my day started. I quietly unlocked the door to my office and slipped inside, making sure the door closed behind me. After putting my purse away, I sat at my desk and turned on my computer and began checking the long list of to-do items I was tasked to complete within the next eight hours: insurance verifications, medical record requests, patient referrals, in addition to the waiting voicemails and phone calls to return. It was going to be a long day.

"Yeah, tea ain't gonna cut it. I'm definitely gonna need something stronger." I sighed, taking out my phone and tapping the DoorDash app. As the tiny feeling of guilt crept up and Karima's voice popped in my head, I reasoned with myself, "I'm only getting iced coffee with Splenda and cream. That's better than a white chocolate mocha frappé with extra whipped cream."

After placing my order, I decided to check my social media accounts starting with Instagram. Like most people, I enjoyed being able to stay connected to my family, friends, and sorority sisters. I loved checking out the latest fashion looks from full-figured influencers and the glimpses into the lives of my favorite celebrities and getting all of their "tea" from the gossip pages provided me a daily dose of entertainment.

But as much as a blessing the popular app was for me, it was also a curse. It also gave me the opportunity to secretly stalk people from my past. Well, "stalk" was the term Karima used. I didn't consider checking on the well-being of someone "stalking," and that word had such a negative connotation. I definitely was not one of those psycho chicks who were obsessed with their ex. But I admit, I couldn't resist temptation.

Don't check it. Don't check it. The only thing you need to look at is the workout of the day from Black Girls Working Out, your horoscope, and confirm that Drake is still single, that's it. Nothing else matters.

The invisible angel on my right shoulder who often served as the voice of reason was ignored as I opened the search box and typed the name then hit enter. Instead of the IG page popping up, I got a message telling me, no user found.

Damn, I must've typed the name wrong, I thought as I retyped the name again, this time spelling each letter aloud as if I were in the final round of the Scripps National Spelling Bee.

"At r-e-g-g-i-e s-p-o-k-e 2-m-e." I hit the submit button again. The results were the same. "What the hell?"

I was about to enter the name a third time when there was a knock on my office door.

"Come in," I said and put my phone away.

"Good morning, Sierraaaaaa." Isis, one of the nurses, entered. "I have a package for you."

"Wow, that was fast," I said, reaching for the venti cup she was extending toward me.

"I didn't even know you were here. The delivery driver rolled in and said it was for you, and I was confused for a minute." She smiled at me. "I ain't even see you come in."

"I've been here a minute," I lied. "I ain't see you either."

"Girl, I was probably in the office talking to Sonya. That's my girl, and you know she's new here, so I have to keep her informed of office procedures." Isis gave me a knowing look.

"You mean you had to give her the tea." I smirked.

"That, too." Isis laughed.

Sonya Duncan was the newly hired nursing director for the clinic. From what I'd been told, she was a newlywed who'd moved from New York, and her husband was starting a new business. I didn't exactly know what he did, but she drove a Tesla and carried a Telfar bag, so they weren't hurting for money, that was for sure. I didn't really know her like that, but she seemed nice. One thing I did notice from the start was that she was thick and curvaceous, like me, and she was fly. Even in her scrubs, she seemed well put together, and to me that was important. I couldn't stand a sloppy plus-size woman. Our reputations were bad enough. Just because a woman was larger than societal standards did not mean she had to be unkempt. My entire life I had been larger than average, but I was neat, fashionable, and always on point. I respected anyone else in my plus-size arena who did the same.

"Thanks for bringing my coffee," I said, opening the straw, putting it into my drink, and taking a long sip. The jolt of energy I felt was instantaneous.

"Girl, you know that ain't no problem at all. You know if you ever want me to stop for you, just send me a quick text. I got you. That doesn't apply to everyone around here, but we cool." Isis's smile was enthusiastic. She was right, we were cool, but there was a reason for her excessive congeniality.

A few days ago, Karima had the brilliant idea to try working out before work instead of after. I wasn't enthused at the idea, but I reluctantly agreed, knowing that it wouldn't last long. One morning, I had to stop at the office to grab my Apple Watch, which I'd accidentally left on my desk the day before. I pulled into the back parking lot just in time to see Isis tossing a bag into the back of her car before getting inside. I tried waving as she drove past, and even though there was no way for her not to see me, she pretended not to. I had no idea why she happened to be there at six thirty in the morning, and I didn't care. But she'd been acting a little strange since that day.

"We are cool." I nodded. "Isis, you got an IG account?"

"Yeah, why?"

"I need to check something right quick."

She shrugged. "Uh, okay. Lemme grab my phone."

While she went to get it, I took another long sip of my coffee and anxiously waited. There had to be some kind of mistake. I hadn't done anything to warrant being blocked by anyone, especially Reginald Darnell Black. We were no longer together, and I'd accepted that fact, but we promised one another that we would always be friends. And from my understanding, friends followed one another on social media. This made no sense.

"Here you go." Isis came in and passed me her iPhone with Instagram already open.

"Thanks." I glanced up before I started typing and saw that her neck stretched and her eyebrows raised. I discreetly pulled back a little. "I can't believe that I got locked out of my account. I tried resetting my password, but I don't even remember the email I used to set it up. That was way back in high school."

"Well, that just made me feel hella old," Isis said and backed up a little.

I typed Reggie's name in, and sure enough, his profile came up, confirming what I already knew. As I scanned his page, I found out something that I didn't know. He had a girlfriend. Not just any girlfriend, either. The most recent picture on his page was of him and an Instafamous model and supposed influencer, Carmen Finesse. My heart sank. Reggie and Carmen had known each other since college, and according to him, they were just cool. Now based on the way he was staring into her eyes as he leaned against her, it was way more than that. He looked elated, and for good reason. After all, Carmen was beautiful: smooth skin, shoulder-length hair, and not an ounce of cellulite to be found anywhere on her body. Oddly enough, while Reggie's athletic body was fully covered in jeans, a designer T-shirt, and sneakers, Carmen wore a barely there bikini that left little to the imagination.

"You okay?"

I blinked, then looked up at Isis, who I forgot was there. After swallowing the lump that had formed in my throat, I nodded. "Huh? Oh, yeah, I'm good."

"You sure?" She frowned. "You don't look like you're good."

"I am." I exited Reggie's page, then passed her phone back to her. "I just saw something on my cousin's page that reminded me of my grandma."

"Aw, I'm sorry." Isis gave me a sympathetic look. "I know the feeling. Sometimes when those Facebook memories pop up of my friends and family who've passed on, I can't stand it."

"Yeah." I exhaled. "Thanks again, Isis. I guess I need to go ahead and get to work. The last thing I want is folks blowing up the office phone and complaining to the director because their record requests haven't been done."

"People make me sick with that. That's another reason I'm glad Sonya is the new manager. She ain't like the old director. I'm telling you, she's cool."

"I hear ya. But I don't know her like that, and I don't even want to have a reason to find out." I forced a smile, hoping it would bring an end to the conversation and Isis would leave. I needed to be alone, and the only reason I felt the need to chat anyway was to use her phone, which I really did appreciate despite the devastation it caused me.

"Well, have a good day. If we order out for lunch, I'll let you know," Isis said on the way out.

"Can you make sure you close the door?" I said.

She nodded and pulled the door closed behind her. When she was gone, I took out my phone, and within seconds, I was staring at Carmen's IG page. Sure enough, there was another photo of her and Reggie, this one at a restaurant, and she was feeding him cake on a fork. Chocolate, his favorite. I then went to her stories and suffered through short video clips of them kissing, walking hand in hand along the sidewalk, and him carrying her on his back. They were a couple. That was why I was blocked. The man I thought was the love of my life was now in love with someone else.

Don't cry. Don't cry. This might not even be that serious. She's all about clout for the camera, so chill until you talk to him. There's no need getting upset over something that may very well be nothing.

I clicked out of the app and gave Siri instructions. "Siri, call Reg."

"Calling Reg cell," Siri alerted me to make sure I knew that she was doing what she was told.

I closed my eyes and waited. The last time we'd spoken was a few weeks earlier when he'd supposedly butt dialed me by accident in the middle of the night. Our conversation was brief, nothing special, but he did mention that it was great talking to me.

"The person you're trying to reach . . ." the operator stated before the phone even connected.

I hung up and decided to send a text instead, causing myself even more disappointment because it was undeliverable. Not only had Reggie blocked me on social media, but he'd blocked me from his phone as well. I was beyond sick at this point and thought about leaving for the day. I glanced at the to-do list again and thought about how much additional work I'd have if I took the day off. I was the only one in my position in the office, and although there was always the possibility of calling in a temp, it was last-minute and really wasn't worth the hassle.

Instead, I decided to use my workload as a distraction. I plowed through the tasks, but it didn't help because all I could think about was how Reggie was now with Carmen, when less than six months ago, he was in bed with me.

Chapter 2

The door I eased in when I arrived to work late was the same one I used to sneak out early. I didn't care if anyone saw me or found out. I'd been cooped up in my office all day and even worked through lunch, so I deserved to leave. I was hungry and angry, meaning I was hangry, and the longer I remained at work, the worse my attitude became. I knew it was time to go when I inadvertently snapped at Kelly, one of the nurses, for a simple mistake that anyone could've made.

"Hey, Sierra, did you get the authorization for Katina Tyler?" she called and asked.

"Who is that?" I began sifting through the insurance authorization requests I'd spent most of my morning completing.

"I requested it two days ago. It should've been done."

"Are you sure? I don't see it, and I've done all of them through today." I checked again.

"I'm positive," Kelly replied. "I'm looking at the email doc right now."

"Forward a copy to me and—"

"Oh, wait, the name is Katina Miller. I found it."

"Great. I'd appreciate it if you'd make sure you have the right name next time before you call and accuse me of not doing my job," I snapped after a brief silence.

"Excuse me?"

I could tell from the sound of Kelly's voice that my rebuttal had caught her off guard, and I didn't really care.

Still, I tried to be a little less abrupt with my answer to her question, but it wasn't any better.

"I'm just saying double-check before calling next time, that's all," I told her before hanging up.

That was my signal that it was time to shut it down for the day. I turned off my computer, grabbed my things, and clocked out. I didn't even want to chance having anyone else call or enter my office.

"Where are you?" Karima asked when she called an hour later.

"Leaving Total Wine and about to go to pick up dinner," I said matter-of-factly.

"What? Why are you getting wine and food when you're supposed to be here at the gym with me?"

"Because I don't feel like working out. I wanna get drunk and eat." I put the bag holding the four bottles of wine I'd just purchased into the trunk of my car. I didn't plan on drinking all four, but there was a strong possibility. "Is that a problem?"

"Yeah, and so is your attitude. What the hell is wrong with you? Did something happen at work?" Karima's concern aggravated me even more.

"More like something happened when I got to work."

"Girl, what? Did the new manager lady say something because you were a few minutes late? I hope not. I hate when new management tries to flex like people are supposed to be scared of them."

"Nah, no one even knew I was late."

"Okay, that's good, right? So what the hell happened?"

I got into my car before answering. "Well, I got on IG and was shocked to see that Reggie blocked me."

"He what? Oh, my God." Karima sighed. "He's an ass. But you know that already. Real talk though, Si, I told you to stop checking his page months ago."

"It's not like I checked it that often," I lied. I didn't check it daily, but I definitely looked him up once a week. "And it's not like I still follow him, so I don't like any of his pics or posts."

"But, Sierra—"

"I know about him and Carmen, Karima," I blurted, sparing her from giving me the all-too-familiar lecture about my needing to let go. She needed to know that this was about more than being blocked. "Why the fuck didn't you tell me, Karima?"

Her silence confirmed what I suspected.

"I can't believe you didn't say shit to me about this," I yelled.

"Sierra, I . . . I mean, I didn't want to make a big deal out of it, I guess. It wasn't my business to tell." Karima's usually loud, strong voice was now soft and timid.

"What? Karima, don't play me like this. I get it. Reggie's your cousin and all, but damn, I'm supposed to be your best friend. This is the kind of shit you're supposed to tell me."

"Look, I told both of you before you started dating and after y'all broke up that I wasn't going to be caught in the middle of anything. He's family and so are you. I don't go telling him any of your business."

"I don't have no business to tell!" I pointed out. "All I do is go to work, the gym, and home."

"That's your choice, Sierra. I invite you out all the time. You're the one who wants to sit home alone instead," Karima replied.

"Because I'm tired from working and going to the damn gym!" I roared back at her. "Do you know how I felt when I saw those pictures of him with her? I was blindsided."

"Sierra, I know you're hurt, but if you hadn't gone snooping on his page, you wouldn't have found anything."

Karima's words stung. I thought she'd be apologetic or at least acknowledge that she should've given me some kind of heads-up. Instead, she was blaming me as if I had done something wrong. I was the one who'd been wronged.

"You know what? You're right. Today has been quite revealing, and I've seen enough. And now I'm going home to be alone as you pointed out," I said, then ended the call.

I managed to hold on to my tears as I picked up my food, got home, changed into my pajamas, and poured a glass of wine. My favorite neo-soul playlist served as the background music as I settled on the sofa, plate in hand, and finally, I allowed myself to cry. Maybe Karima was right. The relationship between Reggie and me ended over a year ago. And I wouldn't have been checking for him, but he was checking for me too. He let it slip the last time we'd seen one another. Four months ago, Karima's sister's wedding provided the perfect setting for our brief reunion.

"Damn, you're looking good." Reggie smiled at me as we stood at the hotel bar.

I tried to play it cool. "Thanks. You too."

It was the first time we'd seen one another since our breakup. I knew I looked flawless. Knowing that he'd be at the wedding was the motivation I needed, and I'd been working out consistently and lost a few pounds. In addition to what I'd hoped would eventually be my revenge body, I'd made sure my dress, hair, and makeup were perfect. At the time, I was more concerned with making him regret breaking up with me, and reconciling wasn't even something I was thinking about.

I casually took my drink and went back to my table. I glanced at the head table as I passed by, where Karima was seated beside the best man. I wanted to make sure she saw that I was on my best behavior and not pressed. She gave me a slight nod.

After the toast was given, the bouquet tossed, and the cake cut, the real party began. The deejay quickly changed the soft, romantic jazz tunes to familiar songs that drew guests to the dance floor. I was pretending to be fascinated by something the guy sitting beside me was saying when Reggie walked over and leaned into my ear.

"Can a brother get a dance?" he whispered over Waka Flocka rapping about how much he enjoyed ladies dancing with "No Hands."

I glanced over my shoulder, giving him a surprised look. "Which brother?"

Reggie smiled and extended his hand. I paused before taking it, then allowed him to lead me to the dance floor. As we danced, I gave in and allowed my mind to acknowledge how damn good he looked. His suit was custom fit, his shoes and tie were both designer, and his haircut was fresh. He looked better than the groomsmen. Our bodies moved closer, and the smell of his Armani Prive Bleu cologne enticed me. It felt good to be near him again, and the magnetic energy between us was still there.

A few more dances and several drinks later, it felt like old times. It didn't take much for him to persuade me to join him upstairs in his hotel room. Before I knew it, I was drunkenly staring into his eyes while he undressed me before reminding me exactly why it had taken me so long to accept our breakup. The sex was amazing.

"Please don't tell me you fucked him," Karima pleaded the next day. Hung over and in need of food, we met for brunch.

"Fine, I won't." I shrugged as I put Stevia into my coffee.

"The moment I saw y'all dancing, I knew y'all were gonna be on some bullshit." She shook her head.

"It's not bullshit, Karima. It was two friends enjoying one another for old time's sake. And it was a great time. Relax." I sipped from the steaming mug.

"That's what you were supposed to do last night—relax. What happened to, 'I'm over him. I don't care that he comes to the wedding. I'm having a good time regardless'?" Karima reminded me of my words that I'd spoken when it was confirmed that he would be in attendance.

"I did have a good time," I said. *"It just happened to be with him. What's so wrong with that?"*

"Nothing, I guess. Just as long as you know it was just a good time, one night. I don't want you getting your hopes up that this changes anything."

"It doesn't, and I know what it was."

I did know that our brief encounter, as enjoyable as it was, didn't mean that Reggie and I were reuniting, but deep down, I hoped that it would remind him of how good it felt to be with me and that he would've noticed my slightly smaller body. One of the biggest reasons for our breakup after three years was because I'd put on a few pounds—fifty to be exact. Mainly it was caused by the stress of losing my grandfather in the middle of senior year and figuring out life after graduation. Reggie decided that in addition to our long-distance relationship not working, he'd also lost his attraction to me. After being crushed, I convinced myself that there wasn't much I could do about the distance, but I could do something about the weight if I tried. Seeing him at the wedding would be the opportunity for him to see, and maybe, just maybe, reconsider his breakup decision. I'd been wrong. Reggie noticed, enjoyed my slimmer figure, but other than kissing me goodbye and telling me how much fun he'd had, that had been it.

Reggie has a girlfriend. He's moved on. What the fuck am I supposed to do now?

Any other time I'd be asking Karima that question, but she'd proven to be a Judas and definitely proven that her loyalty was to her cousin and not me. All that talk about him being a loser and how I was better off without him was bullshit. She never wanted us to date in the first place. Now I was certain that she probably didn't think I was good enough for him. Carmen Finesse had over 200,000 followers, a thriving modeling career, a perfect body, and she lived in the same city as Reggie. Karima was probably elated that Reggie was with her. I'd lost the love of my life and my best friend in the same day. This was too much to deal with.

This ain't gonna cut it. I'm gonna need something stronger than wine.

I'd poured the last of the first bottle of wine into my glass and was headed into the kitchen to get a shot of tequila before calling my plug for some herbal assistance when my doorbell rang. Thinking it was Karima who'd come over to apologize, I ignored it. It rang two more times. Hoping that maybe she may have brought some weed as a peace offering, I decided to go ahead and let her in.

"Damn, you could've at least called first. What the hell do . . ." I stopped mid-sentence, not expecting to see a scrawny white teen holding a plastic bag standing in front of my door.

"I, uh . . . I'm Jerry with Wild Wing Express." His voice cracked as he held up the bag in hopes that it would confirm his identity.

I stared and frowned. "I ain't order anything. You're at the wrong house."

At that moment, the door across the hall opened, and Moe stuck his head out. His eyes went from me to the delivery guy. "That my order? Wild Wing Express?"

"Uh, yes, sir." The relieved guy didn't hesitate and damn near jumped from my doorstep to Moe's. "Here ya go."

"Is that our food?" said a woman's voice from inside his place. "About time."

"Yeah, I'm getting it," Moe yelled over his shoulder.

"And ask that girl across the hall to turn that sad-ass music down. We tryin'a watch a movie."

Both Moe and the other guy looked at me. I responded by slamming my door. I bypassed my kitchen and went straight into the living room, picking up the remote to my Bose speaker and turning the volume even louder.

"Fuck you and your movie!" I grumbled.

Chapter 3

I thought I was dreaming when the alarm from my phone sounded the next morning. I sat up from the sofa where I'd fallen asleep and looked around. Two empty wine bottles, a shot glass, and the guts of the blunt I'd emptied to roll were on the table, along with half of the takeout I didn't remember eating. I glanced at the time and got myself together enough to grab the trash and take it into the kitchen. Luckily, I didn't have a hangover. Had I not splurged and bought good wine, I probably would've had a headache. Noticing that I had three missed calls from Karima reminded me about Reggie and Carmen. The hurt and anger returned, but it damn sure didn't hurt as much. I didn't have time to really gauge how I truly felt because I needed to get to work. I rushed to shower and get dressed. Late or not, there was no way I wasn't stopping for coffee on the way.

Good morning, Sierra. Can you stop into my office as soon as you get in? Thanks. See you then. Sonya.

The text came across the screen of my phone as I was about to turn into the Starbucks drive-through.

"Damn it." I quickly continued straight instead of turning. Sneaking in late unnoticed was one thing, but I couldn't be late when management was waiting to speak to me. I had no idea what she could possibly need to speak to me about. My position was strictly administrative and hers clinical. But I was still considered her subordinate, so it didn't matter.

Instead of my usual casual morning ride, I broke all kinds of laws as I sped to the office. Somehow, I made it with two minutes to spare. I scanned the parking lot, searching for Isis's car, and when I didn't see it, I sent her a text asking if she'd bring me a grande white chocolate mocha coffee, iced. I didn't give a damn about calories, sugar, or anything other than the fact that it was going to taste good and make me feel even better.

Isis immediately replied with a simple Sure and smiley face emoji.

With my coffee order secured, I went into the building and straight to Sonya's office to find out why I'd been beckoned.

"Good morning, Sierra." She greeted me with a warm smile.

"Good morning." My plan was to be pleasant yet stoic, in case this was about to be some bullshit. My previous experiences with black women in management were either extremely good or hellishly awful. There was no in-between. And there were significantly more horror stories than feel-good tales, for sure. Sonya seemed nice, but so had a few of the other fellow sistas, who'd turned into straight bitches.

"Come on in and have a seat. I promise this won't take that long." She pointed to the empty chair in front of her desk. "I know you got just as much work to do this morning as I do."

"You're right about that." I gave a polite smile.

The first thing that caught my eye when I sat down was the framed photos displayed on her desk, all of them of her and one of the sexiest men I'd ever seen. He was definitely big, tall, and worthy of thickTok, one of my favorite categories to explore on TikTok that featured some of the finest king-size brothers on the planet. From the way he stared at her in every picture, you could tell he was beyond in love, as if the huge rock on Sonya's left hand weren't enough proof.

Okay, sis, I see you. Big, fine man and a big ring. No wonder you're so chipper in the mornings.

"I just wanted to take a few minutes to kinda make sure everything is okay and check in with you." Her voice was as warm and welcoming as her smile, but I was still cautious.

"Everything is fine. I mean, I came straight to see you, so I haven't checked my emails or requests yet. Why? Is something wrong?" I asked.

"Well, Dr. Jenkins was concerned about an incident that happened yesterday that he heard about."

"An incident? What incident? I didn't even leave my office yesterday. As a matter of fact, I worked through lunch." I frowned, thinking this was about me leaving a few minutes early.

"Kelly went to him and stated she felt insulted because you raised your voice at her, then hung up."

I tried to read her face, because there wasn't anything accusatory in her tone that indicated the need for me to be defensive. I was pissed that dumb-ass Kelly would even go to Dr. Jenkins with something like that. I shouldn't have been surprised though. It was typical "Karen" behavior, and one thing I'd learned, white women loved to play "victim," especially in the workplace. And when it happened, whoever was in charge never hesitated to come to their defense. I was contemplating my response. Then Sonya took me by surprise.

"You know, it's unfortunate that she felt the need to go to him with something so miniscule. From what I've gathered, you're one of the most hardworking employees here, and you've always been cordial and eager to assist with anything. I told him that if Kelly felt that way, then the first person she should've gone to was you, and if it wasn't resolved, then she should've come to me."

I stared blankly and immediately felt supported in a way that I'd never been before. Isis was right. This woman was a real one. The level of respect I instantly had for her allowed me to be transparent and honest about the situation.

"First, thank you for letting me know about this. I appreciate your being straightforward and direct as well. I respect you for that." I sat up and moved to the edge of my seat. "I do want to be clear about what Kelly is referring to."

Sonya nodded at me. "Please do. That's why I invited you in to talk. Be as clear as you'd like, Sierra. This is a safe space."

"At no time did I raise my voice at her. She called me at the end of a long day asking about an authorization that she couldn't locate and insinuated that I failed to complete it. Turns out, it was an error on her end. I admit I was a bit abrasive and short, but that was after she realized her error and failed to offer an apology," I told Sonya, then admitted, "And I might've hung up without giving a formal goodbye. But she'd already stated she found what she needed, and I'd said what I needed to say, and as far as I could tell, the conversation was over."

Sonya looked at me for a moment without saying anything. Nervousness began to creep in, and suddenly I felt hot. I wondered if I'd been premature in thinking I could speak freely. Then her mouth twitched a little, and her eyes widened. I was confused until a giggle escaped from her mouth.

"Now you know you hung up on that girl." Sonya laughed.

I couldn't help but to laugh as well. "I promise I didn't mean to. It happened so fast, and like I said, it was a long day."

"I get it. She said you left early, too, but she told that to someone else, not Dr. Jenkins." Sonya shook her head. "But don't worry about that."

"She what?" I gasped. "I left a few minutes early because I worked through lunch."

"It's fine. I assured Dr. Jenkins that I was certain this is all a misunderstanding, and it is," Sonya reassured me. Then she lowered her voice. "This conversation isn't about anything that you did. It's about what was said about you. You deserve to know, and as management, I won't allow any of those conversations to take place and not tell you about them, either. That's poor leadership. That's not how I handle my staff."

"Wow, Isis was right."

"About what?" Sonya asked.

"You really are cool. I mean, in a professional kinda way, of course. I don't even know what to say other than thank you."

"I'm just doing my job, and not just the one I was hired to do. We gotta look out for one another because there are plenty of 'Kellys' out here. Thanks for meeting with me this morning."

"Thank you for the chat. I enjoyed it." I smiled as I stood to leave.

"Sierra, I do need you to do something though."

"What's that?" I asked.

"As difficult as this may be, I'm going to need you to be unbothered by this situation."

"Oh, don't worry. I wouldn't dare give Ms. Kelly the satisfaction of having me act funny, nor unleash the cussing out she deserves. I know how the game goes." I winked.

"I know you do, Sierra. Listen, my door is always open if you wanna chat about anything. And next time you wanna tip out early or sneak in a few minutes late, give me a heads-up." She winked back at me.

"I will." I gave an embarrassed shrug.

"Isis was right about you too. You're cool with a good head on your shoulders." Sonya began walking from around her desk, and my eyes went back to the photos.

"You and your husband look so happy," I commented.

"We are. Girl, I'm so in love that it's sickening sometimes, but I don't care. Honestly, he's even worse than I am."

"You're lucky. There aren't a lot of them out there like him."

"I'm blessed, and they're out there looking. You just have to be ready and willing to be found by the one who deserves all that you are." Sonya put her arm around my shoulder. "Oh, and don't settle for anything less."

Sonya's words resonated with me for the rest of the day, and I couldn't get them out of my mind. *"Don't settle for anything less."*

Maybe I've been looking at this all wrong. Could it be that I deserve better than Reggie? I can't imagine loving anyone or being with anyone better than him. He was all that I'd ever desired and more. Hell, truth be told, when we first started dating, I thought he was out of my league.

Instead of working through lunch, I went and grabbed a sandwich from Panera and ate in my car. Karima hadn't called, but she had sent a text saying we needed to talk. Where was that same energy to talk when she found out about Reggie and Carmen? She damn sure wasn't tryin'a talk about that. *Nah, we ain't got nothing to talk about.*

"Sierra!"

I looked up at the sound of someone calling my name and saw Isis waving at me as she walked toward my car. Even though I didn't feel sociable, I reminded myself that she had been generous enough to grab my morning coffee and told Sonya some nice things about me.

"Hey, Isis, what's good?" I rolled down the passenger window, thinking this would be a brief conversation.

"Nothing. What's good with you?" Isis opened my car door and sat in the passenger seat like we were about to roll out.

"Uh, nothing. Finishing up my lunch and about to head back inside," I replied as I reached for my purse in the back seat. "Oh, I need to pay you for this morning."

"Girl, you don't owe me nothing. I got enough Starbucks points to treat the whole staff for a week if I wanted. You're good." Isis waved her hand toward me. "I heard what Kelly did. She's a hot mess. You know why she did that, right?"

"Because she's a white woman?" I stated the obvious.

"No, well, yeah, that, but also because she wants to transfer to the main hospital where her boyfriend works, but she's under contract. She's looking for a reason for them to release her." Isis nodded. "Trying to be slick and throw you under the bus at the same time."

"You're right. She's a hot mess. It's cool though." I shrugged.

"Sonya said y'all had a great talk though. She really likes you."

"I like her too. She's cool, just like you said she was."

"She gave you some good love advice, too, huh? I didn't know you were single. I thought you had a boyfriend." Isis looked surprised.

"'Had' would be the right word." I sighed. "But no, I'm currently not in a relationship."

"Are you dating?"

"No, not dating either," I confessed.

"Girl, why not? You're smart, beautiful, educated, and a great catch. You should be out here getting all the free meals and drinks in the city." Isis laughed.

"Nah, I don't think I should be doing that," I told her. "That's not really my style."

"Style? What the hell does that mean? You don't enjoy being treated like a lady?"

"I'm not saying that. I definitely enjoy being treated right and expect it from my partner, but I can buy my own drinks and meals," I explained.

"No one said you couldn't. You can be independent and courted at the same time." Isis laughed. "And how do you expect to find a partner if you don't date?"

I didn't have an answer because I really didn't have any true dating experience. Reggie was the second guy I'd dated, the first one being my high school sweetheart. There were no in-betweens. Unlike some of my friends, I didn't have a "ho phase" in college. When I wasn't boo'd up, I was hitting the books and simply enjoying hanging out in group settings. The thought of dating someone I didn't know made me slightly uncomfortable, and I felt that women who went out with strangers for free food and drinks gave off gold-digger vibes. That definitely wasn't me.

"I don't know." I shrugged. I'd met both of my exes through happenstance, not dating. "The universe will put us together, I guess."

"Or you can try a dating app. I'm just saying." Isis laughed. "There's plenty of them out there."

"I'll keep that in mind." I sighed, knowing that would be the last thing I considered doing. "But I need to get inside before Kelly runs and tells someone that I'm late coming back from lunch."

"I wish she would. Ain't nobody scared of her, and she don't run shit around here. And if she says anything about you again, I'll personally cuss her out on your behalf," Isis promised.

I wanted to think that she was joking, but somehow I knew that she wasn't. As we got out of my car, I couldn't help but smile. The lunchtime conversation had been the second random encounter with someone I wasn't close to that had a positive impact. My day had gone much better than I anticipated, and I realized I felt better.

Maybe the universe is trying to tell me something. Could being open to meeting strangers be exactly what I need? Should I put myself out there? Clearly Reggie didn't want me, and being the "good girl" didn't work out too well either. I'd been loving, faithful, supportive, honest, and everything else he needed, but it still wasn't good enough. Maybe being committed to one man was a mistake. There was only one way to find out.

Chapter 4

The first thing I spotted when I pulled into the parking lot of my condo two days later was Karima's car. I shouldn't have been surprised to see it sitting there, but I was. One thing about my bestie, she hated being ignored and was going to speak her mind no matter what. There was only so long that she was going to allow me to give her the silent treatment. It took everything within me not to turn around and leave. I pulled into my space and sat in the car for a moment before getting out and going inside, where I knew she was waiting.

"You do know this is breaking and entering, right?" I said when I walked into the living room, where she was lying in her favorite spot on my sofa under a blanket.

Karima looked away from *Wild 'N Out* on the TV screen and cut her eyes at me. "It's not unlawful entry when the owner gave you a key."

"Well, I guess the owner needs to get that key back then," I sneered.

"Yeah, right. We both know that shit ain't happening." Karima went back to watching television as if she were an invited guest. The dress slacks, blouse, and heels she had on was a clear sign that she'd come to my place right after work and skipped the gym, something she never did. She was really pressed to have this conversation.

I put my purse on the countertop of the breakfast bar and continued into the living area. "What the hell are you doing here, Karima?"

After picking up the remote and muting the TV, Karima stared at me. "Don't act dumb, Sierra. You know I'm here so we can talk this thing out. You've given me the silent treatment, and I gave you plenty of time and space to process and calm down. Now let's go ahead and hash this thing out and get back to normal."

"Normal? Is that what it's called when your best friend withholds pertinent information and makes you look like a fool?" I asked.

"How the hell did I make you look like a fool? Wait, what makes you even look like a fool?" Karima frowned.

"Because you knew he was dating her, and you didn't say anything. I had to find out via social media, and the only reason I found out was by using someone else's account because he blocked me. That's foolish!"

"That's stalking, Sierra, and that's on you, not me. I've told you time and time again to stop doing that. You and Reggie have been over for a while. It was pointless. You wanna be mad at somebody, be mad at yourself, not me." She shook her head. "And before you say it, I already know that he might've said and done some things to give you this false sense of hope, and he's dead wrong for that. But again, that's on him and not you."

"You could've at least told me he was dating, Karima."

"And what difference would it have made if I did that? You would still stalk him. I didn't mention it, and look, here we are. You found out anyway. It wasn't my place to tell you," she insisted. "I get it. You're hurt and upset. I'm sorry about that, Sierra, but it's not my fault. I love you and have always been there for you, and I always will. We ride or die for each other, and that has nothing to do with Reggie or anyone else. I was your bestie before him, and I still am."

I folded my arms across my chest and fought the tears that were starting to form. Even though he'd made it clear that he no longer wanted to be with me, I still hadn't let Reggie go. He knew this and used my failure to fully accept our breakup to his advantage at the wedding, but I'd allowed it. I wasn't blameless in this. I hated to admit it, but Karima was right about a few things. I was hurt and upset. I had also been the one attempting to keep tabs on Reggie. More importantly, she'd proven time and time again that she was my closest friend. I trusted her with not only the key to my place, but my life.

"I can't believe he's with Carmen Finesse," I blurted out as my tears made their way down my face.

Karima jumped up and put her arms around my neck. "This ain't about him or who he's with, Sierra. I keep telling you that you deserve so much better than Reggie, cousin or not. You're so focused on him, and that's the problem. Truth be told, I'm glad he blocked you on everything. That's the one good thing he's done."

"What?" I took a step back and blinked.

"It is. Now you can stop worrying about him and focus on yourself."

"I have been focusing on myself. Why do you think I've been working so hard these past few months? I lost almost thirty pounds, in case you forgot," I reminded her.

"You have and you look incredible. But let's be real. You lost thirty pounds because Reggie mentioned that you gained weight." Karima glared at me. "And the moment you found out he was with Carmen, you stopped. At first, I was unsure if you were doing it for him or you, but now I know."

"I did it for me, Karima."

"Then why is it the moment this shit happened, you quit? You stopped coming to the gym, and you've been eating horribly and drinking." Before I could object, she held up her hand and told me, "I saw your trash."

Knowing I'd been busted, my only response was, "I'm taking my damn key back."

"You're not." Karima flopped back down on the sofa.

I slipped off my shoes and took my usual spot on the opposite end. "So you're really not gonna apologize?"

"For what?" She gave me a confused look.

"For not telling me about Reggie and the InstaThot."

"Hell no, I'm not. You're the one who should be apologizing to me for keeping me on read all week."

I rolled my eyes and loudly exhaled, "Fine, my bad. Now that that's out of the way, lemme tell you about my week."

"Wait, before you do that, shouldn't we toast to us making up?" Karima sat up and asked.

"You're not slick, Karima. You saw my damn wine in the fridge, didn't you?" I grinned.

"I may have spotted it," she said with a smirk.

"Didn't you just scold me about drinking this week?" I pointed out.

"This is a special moment between besties, and it calls for an exception." She stood. "We should probably enjoy those chips and guac you have, too."

The two of us went into the kitchen, and as I opened and poured the wine, she grabbed the bag of tortillas that were on top of the fridge and the container of guacamole from inside. And just like that, we were back to laughing and chatting about everything that happened over the past few days. I told Karima all about Sonya's chat about Kelly and her words of encouragement, along with Isis's suggestion that I try online dating.

"I think that's a great idea. I told you months ago you need to get out there. Why you wouldn't, I don't know."

Because I thought your cousin was going to come to his senses and love me again, that's why. I thought he'd realize he was still in love with me the same way I was in love with him. Why did you think I wouldn't?

"I guess I wasn't ready," I told her. "But now I am."

Karima's eyes widened. "What? Are you for real? I don't believe you. Seriously?"

"Why not? He's moved on. So should I." I said the words I'd been thinking all week.

"Prove it." Karima raised an eyebrow at me.

"What? How?"

"Let's go out tonight. One of the guys from work is having a party at Taboo. I'm on the list."

Taboo was a private, invitation-only membership club in the city that catered to local celebrities, athletes, entrepreneurs, artists, and creatives. Anyone who was anyone was a member, as were those who considered themselves elite and could afford the fee of $200 per month. It was a cool spot that was a space for people to have business meetings or work remotely by day, but at night, especially on the weekends, it was the place to be. Karima wasn't a member, but she somehow always managed to be on the list. And though she'd invited me several times, I'd never been.

"I don't know about that. I was thinking maybe we'd hit happy hour at Applebee's or somewhere," I said.

"What are we, in undergrad? Girl, we are hanging with the grown folks tonight. Go shower and get changed. Meet me at my house in an hour." Karima jumped up.

"Wait, are we really doing this?" I began to panic.

"Hell yeah, so make sure you get cute," she told me. "We wanna make sure the fellas know you're on the market when they see you."

Before I could even process what was happening, Karima had hugged me and was out the door. There was no turning back now. Me and my big mouth. As usual, there were no baby steps with my best friend. She was the epitome of all or nothing, and helping me jump into the world of socializing was no exception.

*I'm going to Taboo on a Friday night. I don't even
know what "cute" means when it comes to a place like
that. Applebee's cute, I understand, but I'm sure it definitely isn't the same at Taboo. I know I said that in order
to get something I'd never had, I'd have to do something
I'd never done, but this damn sure ain't what I meant.*

"Sierra, I said get cute." Karima groaned as she got into
my car.

"This is cute." I looked down at the cute white blouse
and favorite jeans that I'd settled on after taking damn
near everything out of my closet. I hadn't really shopped
since losing weight, and most of my clothes were a little
baggy. The jeans still fit tight enough to show off my
curvier ass, thanks to the hundred squats I did daily.

"It's cute if you're going to a parent teacher conference."
She sighed. "Lemme see your shoes."

I moved my feet so she could see the colorful stiletto
pumps I had on.

"Well, your shoes are fly, so I guess that's something.
You got a nice beat on your face, too, and I like the updo
braids." She gave a slight nod of approval. "Come on, we
need to get there. I ain't standing in line."

The closer we got to Taboo, the more nervous I became.
By the time I parked, I was damn near shaking. Before
we headed to the entrance, Karima quickly tied my
blouse at the waist and unbuttoned most of the buttons.
I caught a glimpse of my reflection in the mirrored building and saw that her trick made my waist appear smaller
and my ample cleavage way more visible. My confidence
improved slightly. Instead of standing in the line that
was forming outside the door, we continued inside as if
we were VIPs.

"Karima Stokes," she announced as she passed her ID to the tall, gorgeous woman standing behind the counter at the entryway.

The woman took the license and typed on the keyboard, then looked at me. "And you are?"

"Oh, Sierra Boyd." I reached into my clutch, took out my license, and gave it to her.

"I don't see you on here," the woman said.

"She's my plus one," Karima stepped up and said.

"I don't see where you have a plus one." She handed both of us our licenses.

My heart began pounding. I could sense the anxiousness of the people behind us. "It's cool, Karima. I can go."

"No, you can't. You're my ride home. I can just call Semaj and tell him"—Karima leaned closer and read the woman's name tag—"River here said I don't have a plus one. He'll handle it."

I had no idea who Semaj was, but River's attitude quickly changed. "You don't have to call him. You two can go ahead in."

"Are you sure?" Karima gave her a fake smile.

"I'm positive." River gave her one just as phony.

Karima grabbed my arm and led me through the security gate. Once we were past earshot, we began laughing.

"Who the hell is Semaj?" I asked.

"Girl, one of the owner's sons who's been trying to holla at me for the longest. I don't even know his number." Karima giggled.

"What? And what were you going to do if she had told you to call him?" I balked.

"Called someone and pretended they were him, I guess. Hell, I don't know. The point is, I ain't have to call him and you are in here. Now come on, let's go to this party and find your next future ex."

I glanced around as we made our way through the venue. It was Black people paradise. Every single person was gorgeous, dressed nice, and looked like they smelled amazing. There was a plethora of tall, fine men and beautiful women. There wasn't a dance floor, but there was a deejay playing music, and people were casually swaying and singing along.

"Sierra, this is my coworker, Marc. It's his party. Marc, this is my bestie."

"I've heard a lot about you." Marc smiled as he shook my hand, and I swore he had the most perfect white teeth I'd ever seen. He turned to the guy beside him and said, "This is my boy Ced."

There was something familiar about his friend, but I couldn't really place it. I knew that I'd seen him somewhere before though.

"Nice to meet you," I said.

"How you doing?" Ced gave me a polite once-over, then locked in on Karima. "So you're Karima?"

"I am." Karima nodded.

Ced didn't waste time moving closer to her. "Marc has been telling me all about you. And I swear, he ain't lie, either. You are gorgeous."

"Thank you."

"Ced here is the lead software developer over at Kona, Inc. He's doing some major things over there, too." Marc put his arm on Ced's shoulder.

"Hey, somebody gotta be the one to make the big bucks, right? It might as well be me. How else am I gonna be able to pay for that LS I drive every day? And let's not talk about the trips abroad. A brother enjoys adding stamps to his passport, you know what I'm saying?"

I tried not to laugh at Karima, who didn't try to hide the fact that she was unimpressed by Ced's bragging. That didn't stop her from allowing him to buy us drinks.

I didn't know how big his tab was, but he kept them coming all night long. It still didn't help get her attention.

"Not feeling ol' boy, huh?" I leaned over and asked. After enjoying a couple of shots and a frosé, I felt obligated to at least discuss the possibility of her considering him.

"You already know the answer to that. I don't do arrogance or conceit, and he's very much both." She shook her head. "And look who he's over there chatting with."

I turned in the direction she was looking and spotted Ced standing at another section. Seated in the circular booth, with a woman damn near sitting in his lap, was none other than my neighbor Moe.

"Birds of a feather." I laughed. "I'm not surprised that they know each other."

"Me either," Karima agreed. "Homegirl is latched on tight. She wanna make sure everyone knows that's her man."

"I'm sure the other chick who was at his house the other night, and the other one who was leaving the other morning, think the same thing. I gotta give it to him—his roster is impressive, and he definitely has a type." I watched as Moe's date tossed her head back, laughing as if she were front row center at a comedy show. Her chest was pushed out so far that her breasts were nearly popping out of the strapless dress she had on. Moe and Ced both seemed to enjoy the view she was providing. "Wait, that's where I know him from."

"Who? Your neighbor?" Karima frowned.

"No, Ced. He was at some party Moe was having, and he came over and asked if I had some trash bags," I said, remembering the incident. I'd been gracious enough to give him a couple of bags, then was pissed the following day when I found that instead of taking the bags to the dumpster, Moe and his guests had put them into my garbage can. It was just another one of many neighborly disputes we'd endured.

Look at him over there acting like he's God's gift. That's why he keeps a steady flow of fake broads: fake hair, fake boobs, fake asses, and fake laughs. He probably couldn't handle a woman of substance if he had the chance to be with one. And the dumb-ass chicks probably had no idea that they were even being played. They all deserved one another.

Ced pointed in our direction, and as Moe looked toward us, I quickly turned away as if I'd said the words instead of thinking them. Besides, I had better things to think about and look at instead of superficial-ass Moe and his plastic bitches. I looked over at Karima, who read my mind, and we smiled at each other.

"Waitress, can we get another round?" she yelled.

The vibe was nice, Marc's friends were cool, and a good time was had by all. As the night went on, I realized the reason Karima insisted on coming to Taboo. She may not have been interested in Ced, but she definitely was feeling Marc. At one point, the two of them were so engaged with one another that they didn't even realize his cake was being brought out until someone nudged him.

By the time the party ended, my buzz from earlier had worn off, and I was tipsy. As we walked to my car, loud giggling caught my attention. As luck would have it, Moe was holding on to his companion, stumbling as she walked in her six-inch stilettos. They stopped at a shiny black Acura, and he kissed her before opening the driver door. He waited until she drove off.

"That was fun."

I'd been so distracted that I almost forgot Karima was beside me. "It was. Thanks for the invite."

"Thanks for coming with me. I told you you'd have fun, and see? You did."

"You were right. I did." I nodded and unlocked the doors.

"You sure you good to drive?" She frowned before getting in. "You seem kinda out of it."

"Girl, I'm fine. Besides, I had way less to drink than you did," I reminded her. "You're the drunk one, not me."

"Damn, you're right." She laughed.

"So what's up with you and Marc?" I asked as I drove her home.

"Nothing. We're just cool, that's all." She giggled.

"You seemed more than cool, heffa. I know you, and I know you like him. Can't say I blame you, because brother man is fine," I told her. "And he seems really nice."

"He is fine and he's nice." Karima sighed. "But I don't know. We work together, and you're never supposed to shit where you eat."

"You can always quit and get another job," I suggested.

"Are you sure you ain't drunk? Because you damn sure sound like it right now." She cackled uncontrollably.

It felt good to laugh with my best friend again. Even though it had been my choice not to speak to her, the few days apart had felt like a lifetime. Going out with her was just the thing I needed to cheer me up. Not only that, but I'd had so much fun that I hadn't thought of Reggie one time.

"What the fuck?" I said aloud to no one.

I'd dropped Karima off and made it back home only to find a car parked in my space. It wasn't the first time I'd seen the Acura. Thirty minutes earlier it was in the parking lot at Taboo. I assumed since the spaces marked VISITOR PARKING were all full, the owner of the vehicle assumed she could just park in mine. I threw my car in park, turned on the hazard lights, and stormed toward my building. It was almost two in the morning, but that didn't matter to me at all. I stood in front of the door across from mine and rang the doorbell several times.

"Yo, what the fuck?" I heard Moe bark just before his door opened.

"That's what I said," I responded with just as much frustration.

His eyes were barely open as he stared at me, and I wondered if he was high. He damn sure couldn't have fallen asleep that fast, especially if the broad from the club was there with him. Between his barely open eyes and the way he leaned his shirtless torso against the doorway, I was almost too distracted to remember why the hell I was there.

"Is something wrong?" he asked.

"Yeah, your guest is in my spot."

"Wha . . . My what?"

"Whoever the chick is who's here visiting, she is in my spot. She needs to move her car now!"

"You're kidding, right?"

"Do I look like I'm kidding? Tell her to come move it or I'll call the tow company to move it for her."

"Baby, who is it?" The same chick sauntered in and stood behind him. Her dress was replaced by the same shirt he'd had on earlier, and it hung open, revealing her naked body.

"The person who owns the space where you parked. Move your car," I told her.

"Are you asking or telling?" She looked me up and down.

"Don't move it and see which one I'm doing," I replied.

"Where are your keys?" Moe asked her. "I asked if you parked in the visitor spot, and you said yeah."

"She lied," I told him.

"They're on the counter." She cut her eyes at me and pointed inside.

"Grab them. I'll move it." He directed the statement toward me as if I was going to be impressed by his volunteering.

"I don't give a damn who moves it," I said. "Her shit shouldn't have been parked there in the first place."

She turned and walked off, then returned with keys in hand. "Thanks, baby."

"This is some bullshit and uncalled for," Moe grumbled.

I moved back as he exited his condo barefoot and shirtless. For a brief moment, the girl and I locked eyes. Again, she turned her nose up and looked at me as if I had done something to her. I didn't know if it was because I was still tipsy or what, but I was amused.

The nerve. This chick risked getting her damn car towed to be with a dude who's fucking her and about four others.

"What's so funny?" she asked.

"I'm just thinking about the other night when you were complaining about my loud music." I grinned.

"What?" She frowned.

"The other night, when the dude brought the wings y'all ordered to my house?" I said. "And you said my music was too loud."

"I don't know what you're talking about."

"Oh, my bad. That wasn't you. That was the other girlfriend. Sorry," I said and rushed back to my car.

Chapter 5

My night out with Karima not only helped my mood, but it also made me realize some things. For starters, I needed to go shopping—something I hadn't done since my weight loss. Damn near everything in my closet was too big. Another thing I realized was that although the guys at Taboo were friendly, they focused their attention on the women in the short, tight dresses and midriff tops, even the curvier ones like myself. I'd never felt comfortable in skintight or revealing clothing. It wasn't that I always wore long dresses and muumuus, but tube tops and bodysuits just weren't my thing. But clearly that's what men liked.

Including Reggie. That's all that this chick Carmen wears.

I stared at the latest photo of her on her IG page. Reggie may have blocked me, but she hadn't. And although I tried not to look, and successfully avoided doing so all week, I gave in to temptation on Saturday morning. There were mainly just promotional photos of her, but there were two pictures of her and Reggie.

Oh, my God, y'all are so adorable. Where did you meet? one follower asked.

Carmen didn't answer, but another follower did. I heard they met on Tinder.

Same. But I think they've known each other for a while and fate matched them on the site, someone else added.

Tinder. That bastard told me he hated dating sites and would never join one. Ain't this some shit? I really was a dummy. He was out here meeting bitches on Tinder while I was starving myself.

I closed IG, and then, before I knew it, I'd downloaded the Tinder app.

What the hell are you doing, Sierra? This is crazy. What is the point?

Ignoring the voice of reason, I quickly made a profile before I chickened out.

Hell, when I said I'm putting myself out there, I meant it.

After it was set up, I went to Fashion Nova and ordered shirts, skirts, bodysuits, and anything else I swore I'd never wear. After my mini shopping spree, I decided I'd been lazy long enough and it was time to get back in the gym. This time, it had nothing to do with Reggie. Well, it did. But it wasn't in an effort to get him back. It was to piss him off. I was going to not only lose the weight but get a man who would make him look like the true bum he was.

"Are you really coming to the gym, Sierra?" Karima groaned when I called her.

"I'm walking out the door now," I said. "You coming or nah?"

"But why you wanna go to the gym on a Saturday morning after we've been to the club?"

"Because you're always telling me I got goals and work to do. And it's not like we were even that drunk," I said. "How you gonna be my accountability partner and when I tell you let's roll you complaining?"

"I'm not complaining. And you do got goals and work to do, but we gotta do this today?"

Someone mumbled in the background. I listened closer for a second then asked, "Rima, who's there with you?"

"Huh?" Karima asked, but I knew I'd spoken clearly enough for her to hear what I'd asked.

"You heard me. Who is that?" I whispered as if whoever she was with could hear me.

"Um, let me call you back," Karima whispered.

"Rima. Karima," I hissed, but she hung up.

Karima being boo'd up with her secret lover meant that I'd have to go to the gym alone. Instead of going to our usual fitness center, I decided to go to the one in the community center of my condo. It was one of the "free" amenities I paid for but never used because Karima insisted I get a membership to the one she belonged to. It was a short walk from my house, and I was happy to find that it was empty when I got there.

I guess folks don't work out on Saturday afternoons. More freedom for me. I placed my workout towel down, put my AirPods in my ears, and after a couple of stretches, I hopped on the treadmill. It didn't take long for me to get into the zone, and forty-five minutes later, when I stepped off, I was drenched in sweat and proud of myself.

I did it. And I didn't even need Karima here with me. Over seven hundred calories burned, and it's not even two o'clock.

I was exhausted, but my workout had given me so much energy that I damn near ran back home. I was in the midst of my slow jog when Moe appeared in front of our building. I slowed to a snail's pace and waited for him to leave, but he stood on the sidewalk, talking on his cell. There was no way I could get to my front door without walking past him.

Maybe he'll be so caught up in his call that he won't see me. Just keep your eyes forward and keep walking.

I took a deep breath and headed directly toward my door. I could feel his eyes on me with each step I took that brought me closer and closer. I pretended not to see him as I stepped on the curb and was almost to the walkway when I heard his voice.

"Hold on, man," he told whoever was on the phone, then yelled to me, "You know that was some bullshit last night, right?"

I continued walking as I responded, "Not my fault your guest doesn't know what 'visitor' means. Her parking in my spot was some bullshit."

"No, her parking in your spot was a mistake. I ain't even tripping about you overreacting about that," he said. "But you telling her about another woman being at my crib, that was some bullshit."

Oh, shit, I forgot about that.

"Somebody needed to put her in her place." I shrugged.

"Excuse me?" He took a step toward me.

I paused, then turned around, trying my hardest to ignore his chiseled chest and arms in the tight white tank top he had on. "That one is a clingy, territorial bitch who thinks she runs shit around here. At least your other 'guests' know better."

"I hope you know she was pissed and left right after that shit." He seemed more confused than angry.

"You're welcome," I said with a smirk, then resumed my jog all the way into my house. Leaning against the back of my sofa, I peeked through the blinds of my bay window, which gave me a clear view of the front area, and giggled when I saw Moe still standing in the same spot, looking like he couldn't believe what I'd just said. He was so typical. I was sure he'd never had any woman speak to him the way I did. But I wasn't one of his "pick me's," and I damn sure wasn't trying to impress him.

My cell phone ringing drew me away from the window. I looked down at my watch and saw the call was from Karima. I grabbed my phone lying nearby.

"Oh, you stopped screwing long enough to call me back?" I answered.

"Nobody was screwing," Karima lied, then said, "I'm almost to the gym, so if you coming, come on."

"I'm not coming."

"What? Why not? A little while ago you were screaming about goals and putting in work. I knew you were lying." Karima groaned. "I could've stayed where I was."

"Ain't nobody lying except you. I knew you were boo'd up. And before you tell me who the hell you were laid up with, you need to know I hit the gym already. Check my activity on your watch, heffa," I bragged.

"Oh, shit, you did! Okay, Si-Si! That's what's up. I guess seeing all that eye candy last night put some fire under your ass."

"A little," I said. "But enough about me. Spill it."

"Fine, it was Marc. He invited me over for a nightcap, and I accepted the invite," Karima confessed.

"What? Wait, your drunk ass drove to his house?"

"No, and before you ask, I didn't have him come and pick me up. You know I don't let dudes know where I live. I Ubered."

"You Ubered to his place at two in the morning? You do like him. How was it? Was it worth the ride? And I mean that in more than one way." I would hate for my friend to have paid for an Uber just to end up getting trash dick. That would be tragic.

"We didn't even fuck. We literally had a couple of drinks, chilled, and kinda passed out before it could happen. We did kiss though, and it was like that. So I ain't mad at it," Karima explained.

"What about this morning? You couldn't get it in when you woke up?"

"It's crazy, but we didn't. We just stayed in bed and talked. Then I Ubered home. But check this out: how about I got a notification from Zelle, and he sent me money to cover the Uber? Isn't that sweet?"

"It is. So I guess you decided to shit where you eat after all, huh?" I laughed.

"We'll see. I'm only considering for now. So what are you up to now?"

"About to take a shower, clean up, and see if I matched with anybody on Tinder," I casually said.

"What? You made a Tinder profile? You're lying. I don't believe you. What did you put on it? Never mind. I'm on my way over to see for myself. Hell, I'll even pick up some Starbucks for both of us. We are gonna need some energy for this."

Karima arrived with coffee in hand and didn't waste time taking my phone to see if I'd been serious about my profile. We spent the afternoon swiping left and right and responding to messages from strangers. Some of them were sweet, others were corny, and a few were totally inappropriate. At first, I was a bit overwhelmed by the process, but soon I realized it was no different than weeding out dudes who approached me in the club back in college. The ones who seemed like they had potential to be my type, I would chat with. The others, I walked away from.

"Um, this dude Wes wants to meet up later for a drink," I called and told Karima later that night. He was one of the guys who'd sent me a nice intro message, and we'd ended up chatting on the app for a while. When he asked me for my number, I gave him the Google voice number Karima told me to set up specifically for my online dating. The conversation was pleasant, and he seemed nice enough, but I wasn't sure about meeting him, at least not yet.

"Did you video chat with him?" Karima asked.

"No, not yet."

"Do that first. Then go from there. If he gives a decent vibe, meet up for coffee in the daytime, not drinks," Karima instructed.

"Okay, got it. And I gotta tell you, it's so great having a bestie who's also an online-dating guru."

"Shut the hell up. Just remember, Sierra, you're gonna have to meet more than a few frogs before you get to your prince. Even if you meet up, don't just focus on him."

"I know, I know."

"You know how you get. Don't get caught up too soon. Have fun with this. Keep swiping."

I knew what Karima was insinuating. I even chatted with other guys, but Wes stood out. He was a high school football coach and taught driver's ed. When we chatted on video, he matched his photo, and he was just as cordial as the messages we exchanged. I didn't get any weird serial killer vibes and felt unusually comfortable talking with him.

"Would you like to meet up for coffee tomorrow afternoon?" I asked him.

"Coffee? I thought we would link up and have drinks tonight?" He sounded a little disappointed. "I'm really vibing with you. And I would love to see your beautiful face in person."

I was flattered by what he said, and tempted to agree, but coffee in the afternoon just felt a little safer. "We can vibe over coffee, and I'll still have the same face, I promise."

"Well, I guess if that's what you prefer, we can do that," Wes told me.

And like that, I had a date to get ready for. My first in several years. I was nervous but excited.

Reggie ain't the only one moving on. I am too. A driver's ed teacher definitely isn't as glamorous as an InstaThot, but at least it's a start.

***

"I really had a nice time." Wes smiled at me. "I've never been on a coffee date before."

"It was nice," I agreed as we walked out of the Java Hut where we'd spent the last two hours talking. "Nice" was the perfect word to describe the date.

"I'd love to see you again," Wes told me.

It wasn't that I had a problem with going out with him again. It was just that I knew it wasn't something that I was excited about doing. Wes was a decent-looking guy with a larger build. He was clean-cut and a complete gentleman. But I knew there wasn't any kind of a spark, at least not on my end.

"Let me see what my schedule looks like, and we can talk about it later in the week," I told him.

He gave me a hug that was just as pleasant as the coffee we'd drunk. I allowed him to briefly kiss me on the cheek. After I unlocked my car door, he opened it and closed it after I got in. I waved as I backed out, and before I made it out of the parking lot, I called Karima and shared.

"Well, at least he was nice. That's a good thing. And look at it like this—your first online date was a positive experience. Now on to the next one." Karima laughed.

"Already?" I gasped.

"Girl, yes. I told you online dating is all about mingling. Get out there and have fun."

I wonder how many Tinder dates Reggie has had. Does he take them to the same places he took me when we were dating? Why the hell do I even care? It doesn't even matter. It's time to focus on the dates I want to go on.

As soon as I got home, I opened the app, and sure enough, there were more messages and invites waiting for me. No longer anxious or nervous, deciding who I'd be spending time with next was a little easier.

Chapter 6

"Sierra Giselle Boyd, what the hell is going on with you?" my mother demanded.

"Ma, what are you talking about?" I asked. "And why are you calling me on my work phone?"

"Because you haven't been answering your cell, and when I text you, you act like you're too busy to respond."

"I just texted you yesterday." I reminded her about the brief text conversation we had the day before about a picture of some decorative pillows she was considering for her living room. "I told you the pillows were cute."

"And I asked you another question that you have yet to answer. But either way, I haven't heard your voice in over a week. It's not like you've called to check on me," she complained. "You know, life is short. I won't be around forever. One day you're gonna want to call me, and I'll be six feet under."

Typically, I wouldn't fall for her attempts to guilt trip me, but she was right. We hadn't really had a phone conversation in a few days, maybe a week. Between work, working out, and my new dating life, I really didn't have much time to discuss the latest church announcements, family gossip, or new home decor. In other words, for the past few weeks, I'd been living my best life. My revamped wardrobe was sexier, my Tinder profile was popping with cute pics courtesy of Karima, and my once-dry phone was constantly chiming. I'd gone to more happy hours and meetups than I had in years. Still, none of that was any excuse for neglecting my mother, as dramatic as she was.

"I'm sorry, Ma. I promise I'm gonna do better. But right now I'm at work," I told her.

"I know, that's why I called your work phone. I knew you'd answer." She sighed. "I ain't gonna keep you though. I was just checking on you. I'm glad you're doing all right. Evelyn told me Reggie got engaged. Why didn't you tell me?"

I damn near dropped the phone. Living my best life kept me so busy that I hadn't spied on Carmen's page and had no idea about an engagement. Not only that, but Karima hadn't said anything about it either. Not telling me he was dating was one thing, but I felt like I deserved a heads-up about an engagement.

"Oh, you know what? I guess I kinda forgot." I hated lying to my mother, but it seemed to be a better response than telling her I had no idea. "I will call you later tonight."

"Okay, and respond to my texts, Sierra."

"I will." I quickly hung up.

Engaged. Reggie was getting married. He'd told me he didn't want to be married before turning 30. That was in four more years.

"Hey, Sierra, can you help me find a patient record right quick? It's one of the older ones that hasn't been scanned, and I checked the files in the records room." Isis stuck her head into my office.

"Huh? Sure." I stood up. Feeling lightheaded, I held on to the edge of my desk to steady myself.

"Girl, you okay?" Isis raced to my side.

"Yeah, I got up too fast." I nodded. "I'm good."

"You're sweating. Let me get you some water and a cool towel. Sit." Isis quickly ran out.

I sat back down and tried to calm my racing heart. It wasn't just the news of Reggie that was causing my reaction. The phentermine that I'd gotten from a local weight-loss clinic a couple of days prior was also a factor. I knew the dangers of the pills but still decided to take them, promising myself that it would just be for a little while.

"Here you go." Isis returned with a bottle of cold water and a damp cloth.

"Thanks," I said, taking both. After placing the cool towel on my neck, I opened the water and gulped it.

"You sure you're okay?" Isis frowned.

"Yeah, I'm fine. Like I said, I got up too fast, and I haven't eaten anything today."

"I wasn't gonna say anything, but you really haven't been eating lunch at all these days. That's not good, Sierra."

"I've been doing one meal a day. I'm trying to drop these last few pounds."

"I see you slimming down, but you've gotta do it the right way."

"You're right. And I know better. As a matter of fact, I think I'll take an early lunch. I'll find the file for you when I get back." I opened my bottom drawer and took out my purse.

"Take as much time as you need. Go get lunch and some fresh air. You're good." Isis smiled.

"Thanks," I told her.

When I got to my car, instead of trying to investigate on social media, I drove directly to Karima's office. She worked in a secured building, so I knew she'd have to be called. I'd just walked into the lobby when the elevator doors opened, and she walked out with Marc right behind her.

"Sierra? What are you doing here?" She frowned. "What's wrong? What happened?"

"I, uh . . . I need to tell you something," I said, now feeling embarrassed that I'd come to her job and interrupted her lunch date.

Karima glanced at Marc. "Hey, can you—"

"I'll go grab our food to go. Sierra, you want anything?" Marc offered.

"No, you two go ahead. I'll just talk to you later." I shook my head.

"It's no problem. I'll be right back." Marc touched Karima's shoulder as he walked past.

"Come on, let's go out the side door and chat." Karima took me by the arm and led me out a glass door where we walked to a nice gazebo a few feet away. "Now what the hell is going on?"

"My mom called."

"Is everything okay? Is she sick?" Karima's voice elevated an octave.

"No, she's fine. But she told me Reggie's engaged."

Karima looked just as shocked as I'd been when I heard the news. "What? When? To whom?"

"I'm assuming to Carmen," I told her. "You didn't know?"

"No, I didn't. This is the first time I'm hearing this, Sierra." She shook her head. "I had no idea."

Hearing that made me feel a little better. At least I knew that this wasn't something she was keeping from me like last time. "Oh, well, he is."

"That's wild," she said. "Listen, Sierra, I know what I said before about me not telling you Reggie's business, but I would've told you this."

"Thanks, Rima." I sighed, relieved that she made sure I knew she wouldn't keep something like this from me.

"You okay? I mean, I know that's a dumb question, but still, are you? It's fine if you're not." Karima put her arm around me.

"I'm okay. I'm a little shook, but I'm not devastated. Maybe I'm in shock," I wondered.

"Possibly, or maybe you're over him." She shrugged. "You've been going out, meeting guys, having fun, and putting yourself first. He's finally a non-factor."

Oddly enough, what Karima said made a lot of sense. The reason I'd rolled up to her job wasn't because I was sad about Reggie but more that I was concerned she hadn't said anything. I didn't feel sad or angry to the point that I wanted to cry. I was caught off guard when my mother told me, but I wasn't upset.

"Shit, you're right. I'm over him," I agreed. "Wow, I didn't even realize until now."

"I'm so happy to hear that." Karima hugged me.

"I'm sorry I interrupted you having lunch with your boo. I feel horrible," I confessed.

"It's fine, and he's not my boo. He's my friend." Karima sighed.

She and Marc seemed to be taking things hella slow and keeping it casual. They hadn't even slept together. That alone let me know that she was feeling him. But she was determined not to complicate things.

"Well, let me get back to work, and you and your friend can enjoy at least part of your lunch."

Karima walked me to my car, then said, "We should get drinks tonight. I know I can use one, and so can you."

"I can use a couple," I told her. "You know I'm down. I got a cute new jumper I've been wanting to wear anyway."

"You just been showing out, Sierra. I don't even know who my best friend is these days. I love it." Karima hugged me and I left.

As I headed back to work, I felt a lot better. I ignored my hunger pains for the rest of the day and promised myself I'd eat at whatever bar we ended up at. I rushed home and had just walked in the door when I heard banging across the hallway. I ignored it for a few minutes before finally going to see what was going on.

"Is everything okay?" I asked the chick standing in front of Moe's door.

I've never seen this one before. She must be new. Lord, she barely looks legal. He's picking them younger and younger.

She said, "He won't come to the door."

"Uh, are you sure he's home?" I asked the obvious question.

"I don't know. He's supposed to be." She exhaled.

I walked out and looked at the empty parking space where Moe's car would have been parked, then I told her, "Yeah, he's not home."

"Where is he?" she whined.

"Don't know." I tried not to talk to her like she was slow, but it was difficult. "I think that's probably why he's not coming to the door though."

She looked confused for a moment, then left. It dawned on me that I hadn't seen my neighbor in a couple of days. I'd sort of been avoiding him since our last encounter had been a little embarrassing.

I'd gone on one of my meetups at a wine bar and stayed out a little longer than anticipated. The three glasses of Prosecco I drank without eating didn't help. By the time I drove home, I was exhausted, and as soon as I parked, my eyelids closed. I didn't even know I'd fallen asleep until I heard someone knocking on my window.

"Yo, you good?"

I had lifted my head and turned to see Moe standing beside my car. "Huh?"

"Are. You. Good?" Moe had spoken each word in slow motion.

Awake and now fully aware, I had nodded. Moe opened my door and stood back while I got out of the car.

"Yeah, I'm good," I had told him, and mumbled, "Thanks."

His smirk was visible as I locked my doors and continued what he probably assumed was a walk of shame to my door. Had I not been so tired, I would've taken the time to explain to him that I wasn't drunk, nor was I returning from doing anything inappropriate, not that he deserved an explanation. Since that night, I'd prayed we wouldn't run into one another, and so far, we hadn't.

The hookah lounge that Karima picked for us to meet at for happy hour was smaller than I expected and dimly lit. I tried scanning the crowded bar to find her, but it was damn near impossible. Between the poor lighting and the hookah smoke, I could hardly see. I sent a quick text asking where she was, then decided to wait in a corner near the bar. A few minutes later, she responded.

Got stuck in a meeting at work. Prob not gonna make it.

I was about to leave when I heard my name being called. I didn't see anyone at first and thought I was tripping when I heard it again. This time when I searched for the source, I saw Wes at the opposite end of the bar, waving as he made his way toward me.

"Oh, hey." I waved back at him. We'd talked a few times after our initial date, but I'd made an excuse every time he invited me on another date.

"Fancy meeting you here." He smiled. "You look amazing."

"Thanks," I told him. "So do you."

Telling him he looked amazing was a stretch, but as usual, he looked nice. His outfit was slightly more relaxed: another collared shirt, this one with stripes, and instead of khakis, he wore jeans.

"You're not leaving, are you?" He frowned.

"Yeah, I am. My girlfriend I was meeting can't make it, so I'm gonna go."

"Nah, don't go yet. Look, I got a table right over there. Let me at least buy you a drink first." He reached down and took my hand.

Having no other plans, and not wanting to waste my cute outfit, I decided to take him up on his offer. He led me to his table, which had a hookah setup already in place, and I sat down. When I ordered a glass of wine from the waitress, he tried to get me to order something else.

"That's all you want? Come on now, I remember you told me you like Tito's. Bring her a shot, too. Oh, and bring her a mouthpiece, too," he told her. "You smoke hookah?"

"I do, but—"

"And bring us some hot wings, too, please," Wes told her.

The waitress didn't even look in my direction. I figured she was going to bring everything he told her to, so her tip would reflect it. I checked my watch.

Maybe if I stay for a little while, Karima can still come through after her call at work. I'll text her and hang for thirty minutes. If she can't make it by then, I'll leave.

The thirty-minute window turned into well over an hour, mainly because a trio consisting of a drummer, guitarist, and vocalist who played keyboard positioned themselves on a makeshift stage and began playing. The neo-soul classic songs they performed were flawless, and I was caught up along with the rest of the crowd until they took a break.

"Oh, wow, I didn't realize it was this late," I said, noticing the time.

"Man, it's not even that late," Wes said. "Stay a little while longer. We're having such a good time."

"I have to work in the morning," I said as I stood up. "It's past my bedtime."

"I don't want you to go yet. Ain't no telling when we'll see each other again."

Wes didn't try to hide his disappointment, and I felt a little guilty. I hugged him and promised to give him a call, though I knew the possibility of me doing so was slim. I'd been gracious enough to allow him to move his chair closer beside me and put his arm around my shoulders while we listened to the music.

"It was great seeing you and hanging out," I told him. "You're a nice guy, Wes. I'm glad we're friends."

I turned toward the door and maneuvered my way through the crowd, which was even thicker than when I'd first arrived. I was almost to my car when Wes came running behind me.

"Sierra, hold up," he called out.

I turned around, wondering if I'd forgotten something at the table. My keys were in my hand, and I made sure my phone was in my purse. "Yeah?"

"I'm saying, I really don't want you to go yet. I'm feeling you for real." He grabbed my hand.

Oh God, here we go. I thought I made it clear that I'm not interested in anything other than a friendship, but somehow this dude ain't get the hint. I made sure to tell him I consider him a friend.

"Wes, I'm flattered, I am—"

My sentence was cut off by his attempting to kiss me. I moved just in time before his lips met mine, but he kept his tight grip on me. I realized he was drunk, and I tried not to panic.

"You are so beautiful. I want to take you home with me and show you how much I'm feeling you." He pulled me close.

I tried pulling away. "I don't think that's a good idea. I'm not going anywhere with you."

"You're a tease, and I don't like that shit! You going where I take you!" The gentle demeanor that he had shown was now gone.

"You're hurting me. Let me go!" I barked at him.

"Who the fuck you think you're talking to? I'm sick of you Tinder bitches tryin'a play me for drinks and shit. Nah, fuck that." He began pulling me in the opposite direction of my car. He was so strong that I couldn't get away.

"Let me go!" I screamed as I tried to dig the heels of my shoes into the soft gravel of the parking lot, which was as dim as the inside of the bar.

"Let her the fuck go!" A baritone voice came out of nowhere, causing Wes to finally stop.

"Fuck you. This is between me and my girl, nigga. Keep stepping," Wes growled.

"That ain't yo' girl. Let her go, man." The tall, shadowy figure stepped out, and I saw that it was Moe.

Wes opened his mouth to say something else, but Moe's fist connected with his jaw, causing him to stumble and nearly fall. I took advantage of the moment and snatched away as fast as I could. Wes recovered his balance and reached for me again, but Moe blocked him. Wes flung his large body against Moe's, knocking him to the ground, then climbed on top of him, punching him in the face. Horrified by what was happening, I ran over and kicked Wes so hard that he fell to the side. Moe jumped up and stomped Wes in the chest.

"They fighting!" someone yelled. "Call the police!"

I pulled Moe by the arm. "Come on, Moe. He's done."

Moe glanced over at me, then nodded. "Let's go."

Instead of going to my own car, I ran and got into his, and we peeled out of the parking lot. Neither one of us said anything as he sped through the streets. My heart was pounding, and beads of sweat ran down the back of my neck. Everything happened so fast that I wondered if I was in the middle of a dream.

Moe looked over at me. He was sweating as much as I was, and his eye had started to swell. "You okay?"

I nodded, still too shocked to speak. I'd been moments away from being abducted and, undoubtedly, raped. And the one guy I despised more than anyone in the world had been the one to save me.

Chapter 7

I didn't know how long we'd been sitting in Moe's car. We'd been home for a while, parked in his spot in total silence. I didn't know if he was waiting for me to say something first or I was waiting for him. Maybe we both were trying to think of exactly what to say. The radio wasn't even on. I was certain the sound system in his Infiniti Q60 was state-of-the-art, considering it was a Bose like the one in my Maxima. But I would have to find out another time. Right now, the only thing we were listening to was the sound of our breathing. Oddly enough, it didn't feel weird or strange. It was comforting. My cell phone rang and caused both of us to jump. I silenced the call without even looking at the screen.

"Shit," I finally said.

"Exactly." He nodded. "That was wild as fuck."

"Your eye." I looked at him and gasped, noticing that it was significantly swollen and damn near shut.

Moe leaned forward and stared at his reflection in the rearview mirror. "Damn, I ain't even feel that."

"You need to ice it." I opened my door and got out first. Moe walked behind me and waited as I turned the key in the lock. I entered my condo, expecting him to come inside, but he didn't. I walked back to the doorway, where he was still standing. He gave me an unsure look until I motioned for him to come in.

"Nice place," he said.

"Thanks. We have the same layout. You can go into the living room." I pointed and turned on the main light switch so he could see. While he took a seat on my sofa, I went into the kitchen and grabbed an ice pack out of the freezer and moistened a hand towel. I saw him looking around, and I was glad that I'd cleaned up before leaving for the bar. I kneeled beside him and tilted his head back, carefully placing the towel over his bruised face before laying the ice pack against it.

"Ah." He winced.

"Sorry, it's cold, I know. But it'll help with the swelling." I didn't know what to do first: thank him for stopping Wes or apologize for what happened after he stopped him.

"Thanks," he whispered.

"I'm the one who should be thanking you," I said. "There's no telling what that bastard would've done if you hadn't been there."

"That wasn't your dude." It sounded more like a statement than a question.

"Hell no. That was some clown I met online," I explained.

"Man, you know how dangerous that is? You out here going out on dates with niggas you don't even know? Late at night?" He looked at me like I was crazy.

"That's not what happened. It wasn't a date. I was waiting for my friend, and he happened to be at the bar."

"Oh, so you know him."

"I mean, I met him before. He seemed like a nice guy," I whined.

"Seemed like. So you don't know him." Moe raised an eyebrow.

"No, I guess I don't," I relented.

Moe shook his head. "What's going on with you, man?"

I sat up and turned toward him. "What do you mean?"

"I'm saying, you lost some pounds, and now you're around here dressing different, going out with random-ass dudes, coming home drunk, and passing out in your car. Why?" He took the ice pack from his face and held it.

I stared at him, trying to think of how to respond to everything he said. The fact that he'd even noticed all of that about me was a total surprise. I tried to read his face, searching for an indication that he was joking, but the only thing I saw was genuine concern.

"I wasn't passed out in my car. I was tired from a long day." I wanted to make sure I cleared that accusation up first and foremost. "And I know you're not talking about my dating life. You have so many randoms popping in and out of your place that at one point I thought you were giving out good dick and free sew-ins. Two things they all have in common: you and weave."

Oh, shit, maybe that was too much. I didn't mean for it to come out like that.

Moe stared at me as if he was just as shocked by what I'd said about him as I'd been by what he said about me. Our eyes met. The ends of his lips curled, and then we both laughed. It was as if we were both relieved to get something off our chest that we'd been holding in.

"Well, damn," he said when he finally caught his breath.

"I'm just saying." I shrugged. "Oh, and one of your randoms came by earlier banging on your door looking for you. You should be ashamed of yourself because she barely looks legal."

"What? Who?"

I moved his hand so that he was putting the ice pack back over his eye. "I don't know. I've never seen this one before, so she must be new."

"I don't know who that could have possibly been."

"See, you got so many randoms that you can't keep up with them." I grinned.

"It ain't as many as you think, for real. But back to you. What's the deal? I thought you were different."

"What's different?"

"A good girl with a decent job and cute friends and a boyfriend who baked cookies on the weekends."

"What are you, a stalker?"

"Nah, I'm just a neighbor, same as you."

"Well, the boyfriend is gone, and no one really wants a good girl these days. You of all people should know that."

"Why should I know that?"

"Uh, because you're shallow and materialistic, that's why."

"Whoa, I may be a lot of things, but I ain't shallow." He had the nerve to act offended.

"You're kidding, right? Every chick who crosses your threshold is a size six, wears the same outfits from Fashion Nova, and probably either is an influencer, has a beauty brand, or I'll go so far as to say works as a stripper. You have a type. As long as she looks a certain way, you'll deal with them—temporarily, of course. And you treat them well and make them feel special, so they don't even realize you have no intention of committing to them."

"That's really what you think? That's how you see me?"

"You saw me as the fat-ass good girl who stayed in the house and baked cookies," I said as I stood up. "I'll get you another towel."

"Thanks. And I saw you as the beautiful albeit stuck-up bitch who lived across the hall and always complained about everything, to be honest," he snapped. "And I thought I was wrong."

"And I saw you as the fine yet conceited man-whore with bad taste in women and destined to be a bachelor his whole life, to be honest," I said. "I could be wrong."

"Very." He nodded. "I have great taste in women. Hell, if your ass wasn't so damn mean all the time, I probably would've asked your sexy ass out."

"Liar. You would not." I went to walk toward the kitchen, but Moe grasped my arm, stopping me.

"I'm not lying," he said.

My eyes went from his fingers to his eyes. He must've sensed my mind, because he proved his point by pulling me closer and putting his arm around my waist. Because he was nearly six inches taller than my height of five eight, I had to look up at him. I softly touched his bruised eye, and he held my gaze.

He is so damn fine. I see why chicks stay trying to get at him. This man is pure chocolate perfection.

Even with a swollen face, he was gorgeous. I'd never noticed how thick his brows were. There was something about the way he looked at me. At first, I couldn't figure out what it was. Then it hit me.

Shit, maybe he's not lying. He wants me. Wait, am I tripping? There's no way.

As I contemplated whether I was wrong, we kissed. I didn't know who kissed whom first, and I damn sure didn't care. The only thing that mattered in that moment was the feel of his lips on mine and the sweet taste of his mouth. My arms made their way around his neck as our tongues became acquainted with one another. The kiss was soft at first, but as he gently sucked my bottom lip, the passion grew. My mouth wasn't the only thing that was wet. Moe's hands slipped from my waist and cupped my ass, pushing me against his pelvis as if he wanted me to know the desire was mutual. I decided to go a step further and find out for myself. My fingers fumbled with the button of his jeans and slipped inside. His stiffness grew even more, and I smiled.

"Told you I wasn't lying," he whispered into my ear, making me hotter than I already was.

It didn't take long for him to slip my jumpsuit off my shoulders. I was grateful that I'd chosen to wear one of my new, sexy bras. Before he removed it, he gathered both my supple breasts into his hands and teased them with his tongue through the lace. My nipples hardened, and I moaned as I pushed the jumpsuit over my hips and stepped out of it.

Damn, my girdle. I forgot about this.

I panicked at the realization of the black satin panty girdle I had on and tried to think of what to do. If Moe had a problem with it, he damn sure didn't show it. He dropped to his knees and carefully peeled it off my thick thighs like he was unwrapping a prized possession. I was damn near dipping at this point and especially after I pulled his shirt over his head.

"Damn," I whispered as I stared at his chest.

"You're so fucking sexy, Sierra."

I couldn't wait any longer. I pulled him to his feet and led him into my bedroom. The kissing resumed, and I went to kick off my heels, but he shook his head.

"Nah, keep them on." He pushed me onto the bed and began licking my inner thigh as he slipped my panties off.

I was glad I let Karima bully me into getting waxed. At the time, it hurt like hell, and I thought it was a complete waste of time and money, especially since I had no one I'd even consider fucking. Now it seemed like preparation, and the universe had rewarded me.

"Oh, shit." I moaned as Moe's finger entered my moist center. He positioned himself precisely before using his tongue to please me in ways I'd never had done before. I tried to move, reaching for my headboard as I climaxed so hard that I thought I would never stop, but he gripped my legs so tight and kept sucking on my clit. The torture was pleasurable, and I begged for him to stop. He didn't until I'd nearly drowned him and he was certain that I was satisfied.

"That's what I was waiting on." He grinned.

"I guess reciprocity is in order," I offered, looking down at the bulge between his legs.

"Maybe next round. Right now, I wanna fuck you." He licked his lips and pulled out his hardened penis. Even his dick was beautiful: not too long, thick with a slight curve. I was in for a treat and knew it.

I reached into my nightstand and took out a foil-wrapped condom. I sat up on my knees and kissed his member before slipping on the rubber. Moe reached for me, and we made our way to the center of the bed. We touched and explored one another, and then he positioned himself between my legs. My eyes closed in preparation for what was about to happen. He slowly entered me, making sure I could handle what I was being given. Once he was sure, the tenderness turned to vigor, and we engaged in a sexual escapade full of rhythmic, ferocious intensity. When it ended, we were both exhausted and smiling.

"Whoa." He panted and fell to my side.

"Exactly." I nodded as I tried to catch my breath.

"We've been neighbors all this time, and this never happened. I'm kinda mad at myself right now." He laughed.

"You should be." I giggled.

Sleeping with Moe wasn't even something I ever thought about and never considered was a possibility. I didn't even like him. As he pulled me into his chest, I was glad that I did. It felt like fate. For months I'd been craving good dick, and he did not disappoint.

"Wait, you did what?" Karima screamed the next day when I told her everything that happened. I quickly turned down the volume of my phone and made sure my office door was closed.

"I know, it's crazy, huh?" I sighed, drained and still astonished from the night before.

"I know you're lying, Sierra. That shit did not happen."

"It did, I promise."

"Ain't no way you'd be at work if that happened. I know you." Karima laughed.

"I almost called in," I confessed. But when my alarm went off, Moe got up, so I did too. He told me he had a great time and said we'd talk later, kissed me briefly, then left. "I was worried if I stayed home, I would think about him and watch his house, so I came to work as a distraction."

"Ain't no way you can stop thinking about him after all of that. This dude swoops in and beats up a potential rapist, drives you home, then properly seduces you before blowing your back out? Oh, you're gonna be thinking about his ass for a while." Karima broke down the series of events as if I needed reminding.

"Tell me about it."

"So now what? Do you go back to hating each other, or are y'all cool now?"

"I think it's safe to say that we're cool. I mean, I guess we're cool. He says we'll talk later."

"What does that mean? Later today? Later when you happen to run into each other in the hallway? Is he gonna call?"

I didn't know the answer to any of her questions. I hadn't even thought about them. "I doubt if he'll call. He doesn't even have my number."

"Do you want him to call?"

"Of course I want him to call. I just told you the man sexed me damn near into a coma after saving my life."

"Sierra, that was just sex. At the end of the day, you don't even know him like that. What we do know is that he sexes a lot of women. I'm not tryin'a be funny, but I don't want you to confuse anything and get caught up," Karima said.

"I know it was sex, Karima. And no one is getting caught up. I'm not in love with the guy if that's what you're thinking. But we had a nice time. You act like I'm about to be sprung."

"That's not what I'm saying at all. I just want you to maintain the right perspective. Moe is who he is and does what and who he does. I don't want you to start thinking there's even the possibility of it being anything else."

"I won't." For some reason, I was a little irritated. I knew Karima was trying to be helpful, but she was giving off a vibe that I didn't like. "It happened and we're cool."

"I get it. I think you shouldn't let it happen again. I don't want to see you hurt."

"I don't think he'd do that," I said. "I hear what you're saying, but this was—"

"Sierra, come on. You've seen the women he goes for. The man has a roster of women who are damn near interchangeable. And you don't look anything like them."

"Damn, well, thanks for the vote of confidence."

"That's not what I meant. I'm sure you got to see a more personable side of him, but Moe is for the streets. We both know that. Last night didn't change that. I just don't want you to forget it."

"I won't. I will talk to you after work."

"Gym at five?"

"Yeah, I'll be there," I agreed.

I ended the call, still feeling a little disappointed. What Karima said made a lot of sense. But last night was more than just sex. Crazy as it seemed, although I didn't look like any of the other women, I felt the connection between us.

Chapter 8

Dinner tonight? Knock three times if you accept.

I smiled at the note I found waiting for me on my door when I got home. My first instinct was to turn around and knock three times on the door, but instead I went into my condo. Karima's cautionary advice continued while we were at the gym, and it was all I could think about. I didn't want to play myself or look dumb. And I damn sure wasn't about to be part of the Moe-tel rotation of guests. I was confused, tired, and sweaty from my workout. I couldn't think straight. Seeing Moe wasn't a priority. A shower and nap were.

Knock. Knock. Knock.
I thought I was dreaming when I heard the knocking. My eyes opened, and I listened closely to make sure.
Knock. Knock. Knock.
I got up and slipped my feet into my Crocs, then went to see who it was. I didn't know what time it was, but when I lay across my bed, it was still light outside, and now it was dark. I checked the peephole and saw the back of Moe's head.
"Hello, neighbor," I said as I opened the door.
"Hello to you too." He grinned. "How are you?"
His eye was still very much bruised, but the swelling had gone down a little. He still looked good as hell.

Don't act pressed. It was just sex. Good sex, but that's all.

"I'm good. A little tired. How are you?"

"I'm cool. I just wanted to come and check on you. I mean, under normal circumstances, I would've called or sent a text, but I don't have your number," he told me. "Hence the reason I left the note."

"You left a note?" I pretended as if I had no idea what he was talking about.

"I did," he said with a smirk.

"Interesting, I didn't get a note from you." I leaned against the doorway.

"I mean, I didn't sign my name, but I didn't think I had to. Now that I think about it, maybe I should have." He took a step closer to me. The aromatic scent of his cologne was woodsy, spicy, and expensive, inciting flashbacks of his body on mine.

I fought the distracting thoughts. "Maybe."

"I'll remember that next time. But hopefully you'll just give me your number, and I won't have to resort to paper and a pen. So can a brother get that?" he said with a seductive grin.

"Get what?" I couldn't resist flirting back.

"Whatever you wanna give me." He leaned in closer.

Don't do it. Keep it cool. Act unbothered.

"Okay. Four-three-eight nine-seven-four-two." I blurted the numbers out, then stepped back inside so fast that Moe almost fell.

"Cute." He smirked. "All right, neighbor. Well, I'll get in touch."

"Please do." I nodded, closing the door after he stepped back.

My growling stomach made me wish I'd taken him up on his dinner offer. I went into the kitchen in search of something to eat. Nothing seemed very appealing. My phone chimed with a text.

You coulda at least let a brotha get a neighborly hug.
:-) - Moe, the dude across the hall.

I shook my head, surprised that he'd remembered the numbers. I decided not to text him back. Moments later, I was standing in front of his door, scolding myself for what I was doing.

Knock. Knock. Knock.

"You're right. I can at least give you a hug," I told him.

He pulled me inside and kissed me.

The next two weeks flew by. Moe and I weren't together every night, but we began spending a lot of time together. I decided not to share much of what we were doing with Karima. I told myself if he and I became serious, or anything really popped off, then maybe I'd tell her. Until then, it was my little secret. She had her own situation she was dealing with anyway with Marc. When we talked, I let her monopolize the conversation with how she liked him but didn't want to be caught up in an office romance.

"What's been going on with you? You got any hot dates lined up this weekend?" she asked.

"Not really," I said as we walked out of the gym. "My Tinder matches have kinda dwindled. But I am going out to celebrate Isis's birthday this weekend."

"That should be fun."

"Yeah, it's a whole itinerary of events: spa day, brunch, dinner. You know she's hella extra, but I promised I'd participate." I sighed.

"Your boy tried to get up again?"

"Nah. I mean, we chat when we run into one another, but nothing unusual."

Unless you consider hot sex in the shower then on the bathroom counter unusual. Oh, or the Netflix and chill night that turns into strawberries, whipped cream, and orgasms on the couch.

"Hoes still checking into the Moe-tel on the regular, huh?" Karima joked.

I'd been pleasantly surprised that the female traffic across the hall had not only subsided but was nonexistent. I'd been waiting for someone to pop up or for Moe to tell me he was expecting company or had plans, but he didn't. Even when we weren't spending time together, he was pretty much home alone from what I could tell.

"I think he left for one of his business trips this morning. So he'll be gone a couple of weeks. The Moe-tel is temporarily closed." I shrugged. "He was putting his luggage in the car when I left for work."

I'd been kinda sad when Moe told me he had to go out of town for work. He hugged me and gave me one of the best goodbye kisses, leaving me breathless and wanting to climb into one of his suitcases.

"I'll text you when I land and Facetime you later tonight. Promise me you'll wear something sexy," he'd told me.

"I will if you promise you'll be naked." I'd winked.

I hated that Moe was gone, but Isis's birthday extravaganza plans seemed like they would keep me occupied. I was nervous because I'd never hung out with her outside of work. And other than Sonya, who was also going to be there, I didn't know any of her friends. But Isis assured me that everyone was fun and I was going to have a great time. Also, everything was planned and paid for, and she'd even arranged for transportation.

"You rented a party bus for the entire day?" I asked when I arrived at the designated pickup location.

"I did." Isis greeted me with a mimosa and a hug. "We'll be partying all day, won't we?"

"And all night!" another woman already seated on the bus yelled. Sonya was sitting right beside her. She waved at me, and I waved back.

"That's my sister Jazz. She's a wild child, so be prepared." Isis lowered her voice.

"I heard that," Jazz yelled.

"She and Sonya have been best friends for years," Isis told me, then pointed to the other ladies on the bus. "That's Nikki, Tammy, my other sister Egypt, and you know Sonya."

"Let's go," Jazz yelled.

"We're waiting on Coco. She said she's on her way," Isis replied.

"Man, we're gonna be late to the spa. Tell her to just meet us there. You know she's never on time," Egypt told her.

"I know y'all bitches wasn't about to leave me," a beautiful, curvaceous, brown-skinned woman stepping onto the bus in designer shades announced. "Y'all know better than that."

"Girl, get your ass on the bus so we can go." Isis pretended to push her.

"Sierra, you can come sit over here." Sonya motioned for me.

Karima was worried about dating her coworker, and here I was about to drink and party with my boss. I didn't know what the protocol was for that, but I figured the best thing was to be polite, professional, and be seen and not heard.

I went and sat beside her. "Thanks."

"Don't worry, I don't know any of them either other than Isis and Jazz. But they all belong to a book club. I got a feeling we're about to have a blast." Sonya raised her glass. "Cheers."

"Cheers," I said.

Isis did not disappoint, and neither did her friends. We were treated like royalty at the day spa, then chauffeured to a huge Airbnb they'd rented, where a private chef had prepared a massive brunch buffet. We ate, hung out by the pool, continued drinking mimosas, danced, and sang karaoke. We changed and then went to dinner at Z on 23, a rooftop restaurant at Le Méridien Houston Downtown. The coolest thing was that there was a photographer with us who captured the entire day.

"Oh, shit, that's Carmen Finesse," the young man commented as we prepared to pose for a picture while waiting to be seated.

I held my breath as I looked around. I didn't see Carmen anywhere. *She can't be here. Please, God, don't let her be here.*

"Who?" Isis asked.

"Carmen Finesse. She's some IG model," Coco explained.

"Never heard of her." Sonya shrugged.

"Where?" Egypt stretched her neck to see where the photographer was pointing.

"Over there. That must be her new dude."

I became even more anxious. Reggie was with her? *Shit. Of all the fucking restaurants in Houston, she and Reggie had to be here? Why? Sit down before they see you. Hurry.*

"Nah, I don't think so. That's her old dude," Coco said. "I follow him too, so I know."

"I thought she was engaged." I tried to sound innocent.

"I did too." Coco laughed. "That girl is a mess."

I was no longer worried about being seen. I wanted to see for myself. I casually strolled beside the photographer. Sure enough, hugged up in the far corner was Carmen and a guy who definitely wasn't Reggie.

Wait, did she and Reggie break up? They must have, because his hand is on her ass and her arm is around his neck. The two of them were so into one another that they didn't even realize we were looking. *Take a pic.*

"Table's ready, guys," Isis said.

I took out my phone and tried my best to snap a pic of Carmen and who I assumed was her ex. I tried to enjoy the rest of the night, but I was too distracted. Seeing Reggie's boo with another man was the last thing I expected, and I had so many questions, and I needed answers. I had no choice but to send the pic to Karima, and I told her to call me ASAP.

"Who's that?" she asked moments later.

I excused myself from the table and quickly went into the bathroom. "You know who that is, Rima."

"The picture is dark as hell. I can't tell who it is."

"It's Carmen Finesse, and she ain't with Reggie." I tried not to sound excited.

"Oh, damn," Karima said. "Yo, that's grimy."

"Tell me about it. Did they break up or something?"

"Not that I know of. Hell, I still haven't confirmed that they're engaged. I asked my mom, and all she said was, 'That's what I heard.' You know how my family is sometimes. How's the party?"

"It's fun," I said, more concerned about the possibility of Reggie being cheated on than Isis's birthday. "You need to call him."

"Call who?" Karima asked.

"Reggie, that's who. You should at least find out if they broke up or something. She's here in Houston kissing another man. He needs to know."

"Not my business and not yours either. Stay out of that."

"But—"

"Sierra, you okay?" Sonya walked into the bathroom and asked.

"Huh? Yeah, I'm fine." I nodded. "I just had to take an important call. Rima, I'll talk to you later."

"Okay, they're about to bring out the cake," Sonya said. "Nurse Duncan."

Sonya and I both turned around and looked at the young lady who had just walked in. She looked kind of familiar, but I wasn't sure where I'd seen her.

"Hey, Morgan, how are you? You feeling okay these days?" Sonya asked.

"Yes, ma'am. I know you said the first trimester was the hardest. You weren't lying." Morgan gave her a weak smile.

"It'll get better. Hang in there." Sonya rubbed her shoulder. "It was nice seeing you."

"You too." She nodded and went into one of the stalls.

"We better get out there before we miss singing 'Happy Birthday,'" Sonya told me.

"I'm right behind you," I told her. When we got back outside, I looked back in the corner, but Carmen and the guy were gone. I knew Karima told me to stay out of it, but there was no way I could. Somebody needed to tell him.

Chapter 9

"I mean, I think your friend is right," Moe said. It was late as hell when I finally made it home after the party, but he'd insisted that I FaceTime him so we could talk. I didn't hesitate to tell him about seeing Carmen, expecting him to agree with me instead of Karima. He didn't. "It's not your business."

"Did I mention that Karima's his cousin? I'm not saying that it's my business either. If anyone should tell him, it should be her. That's family," I pointed out.

"True, but if she doesn't want to tell him, then that's her choice," he said as if it were no big deal as he lay shirtless against the headboard of his hotel bed.

"If my cousin saw my significant other cheating with another man, I would want her to tell me. Wouldn't you want someone to tell you?" I asked, slipping out of my clothes.

"Maybe. It depends. Lower your phone. I'm tryin'a see something."

"Focus, perv." I laughed.

"I'm trying to, but you are so concerned with your ex that you won't let me."

I picked my phone up off the bed and stared into it. "What is that supposed to mean?"

"Nothing, but you seem real concerned about somebody who you claim to be over. If I ain't know better, I'd think you were still in love with ol' boy. Are you?" Moe looked at me.

"Hell no, I'm not." I looked at him as if he were crazy.

"I'm saying, if you are, then it's cool."

"I'm not."

"You sure about that?"

"I'm positive, and I'm offended that you even suggested that I am. This isn't even about him. It's about how nonchalant Karima is about the situation. She's a little too unbothered if you ask me."

"Which I didn't." Moe sighed. "You know what? I'm sleepy, and I got an early flight tomorrow. We'll talk when I get home."

"Why the attitude? You're the one who told me to FaceTime you." I frowned.

"Because I thought it would be a chill conversation and you would tell me about the party with your friends. Not that you would have a meltdown about your ex," Moe snapped at me. "Bye, Sierra."

I looked at the phone after he hung up. I couldn't believe he was tripping for no reason. A simple conversation about Karima had somehow turned into an unwarranted accusation and attitude. I tried calling him back, but he didn't answer.

Fine. If that's the way he wants to act, then that's on him. One thing I ain't gonna do is concern myself with someone who technically ain't even my man. Moe is cool, but that was out of pocket.

After tossing and turning all night, I tried calling him the next morning. His phone went straight to voicemail. I figured he was on the plane and headed home. I felt like the conversation had gone left and we'd misunderstood each other. I told myself to wait until he arrived home a few hours later when we could talk face-to-face. I'd been promising to prove to him that I could cook, and I figured this was the perfect time to show off my skills. I got dressed and headed to the grocery store to pick up everything I needed to make a gourmet meal.

***

The crab-stuffed salmon was baked, the macaroni and cheese bubbling, asparagus broiled, and homemade rolls cooling, and Moe hadn't made it home. I also hadn't heard from him. I tried calling him again, but his phone continued going to voicemail. I wasn't sure what time he was scheduled to arrive, but if his flight was in the early morning, he definitely should've been back in the city.

Is he still mad? He can't be. Our conversation was heated, but it wasn't that bad. He still should've at least called.

I waited another hour, then made myself a plate. I didn't even bother baking the chocolate chip cookies waiting to be put in the oven. There was no point. I put the food away and watched television in my bedroom until I fell asleep. No one else was in my thoughts, including Reggie or Carmen. Only Moe.

The next morning when I left for work, his car still wasn't there. I was officially worried. If something had happened to him, I had no way of knowing. I really didn't know any of his friends or family.

"Thanks for joining me and my crazy friends, Sierra." Isis greeted me with my favorite Starbucks order. "And thank you for my beautiful journal. I love it."

"Thank you, and I'm glad you like it. I hope you use it, too." I smiled.

"I promise I will. I wish you had spent the night at the Airbnb. You know we were still turning up when we got back."

"I'm sure you all did." I laughed. "Your friends and sisters are a whole vibe."

"You've gotta join our book club. Sonya is joining too. We're BGBC, the Big Girls Book Club. I know you're around here tryin'a be a skinny Minnie, but you still got plenty of curves, so you qualify."

"I'll think about it," I promised.

When Isis was gone, I sat at my computer and tried to think whether I should call the hotel and ask for Moe's room. I thought about calling the company he worked for and requesting to speak to him. I even pulled up his LinkedIn to see if there was a direct line to his office.

Shit, Karima's right. I'm a stalker. I'm officially doing the most.

I closed the website and started working. I had barely started checking my emails when I heard a commotion. I went to see what was happening.

"Ahhhhh," a woman moaned.

"Get a wheelchair," Sonya yelled.

"I'm on it." Isis came running past my door.

It wasn't uncommon for patients to come into the office instead of going to the hospital when they were unsure if they were in labor. A few times, there had been actual births. I wondered if this was going to be one of those instances. My curiosity got the best of me, and I strolled behind Isis as she pushed the wheelchair to the lobby. The other patients who were waiting seemed to be just as curious about what was taking place as I was.

"It's okay, Morgan. We've got you," Sonya coaxed. "We gotta get you into the chair."

The young woman she was talking to was the same young lady we'd seen in the bathroom at the restaurant. She moaned again as she doubled over. "I can't. It hurts."

"I can lift her."

I did a double take as a set of strong arms took hold of Morgan and gently picked her up. I thought I was tripping and seeing things, but sure enough, it was Moe.

"Thanks," Sonya said. "Let's get her to exam room three."

Isis nodded, and I held the door as she wheeled Morgan into the hallway and to the exam room.

"Is she gonna be okay?" Moe looked scared shitless.

"We're probably gonna have to call EMS and have her transported. I know you brought her in. You can ride with her if you want," Sonya told him.

"Okay." Moe nodded.

"You can wait out here," Sonya said.

Moe began pacing back and forth. I quickly stepped back inside the door so he wouldn't see me. I now understood why he'd disappeared. He was with his baby mama he'd failed to tell me about. I'd been played. I went back into my office and sat at my desk, shocked and hurt. Unable to stop myself, I sobbed.

It took a little while for me to get myself together. When the tears stopped, I went into the staff bathroom. The office was calm, and there was no sign of Moe or Morgan.

Morgan, the mother of his child. Shit, she was a child herself.

I wanted to find out her age, and it wouldn't have taken much to pull up her medical records, but I didn't. There was no point. It wouldn't change the fact that she was pregnant. I took out my phone and deleted Moe's number. Not that I expected him to call me. I was done. That didn't stop Isis from coming into my office with an update.

"What a morning." She flopped into the chair and exhaled. "I'm glad that young lady came in when she did."

"Is she okay?" I asked, not out of concern, but to be polite.

"She lost the baby, but her tube didn't rupture. She could've died."

"Bittersweet, I guess."

"It is. She's young. She has plenty of time to have kids."

"Yeah, and her boyfriend seems supportive," I added.

"He was more scared than she was. He held it together though, and did you see the way he swooped her up and put her into that wheelchair? Superman status," Isis said excitedly.

The tears I thought were over started flowing again. "I'm sorry."

"Girl, what's wrong? Why are you crying?" Isis gasped.

"I don't know. I'm just emotional for no reason. Probably that time of the month," I lied. "And then watching all of that happen."

"I get it." Isis gave me a sympathetic nod.

"I'll be okay. I think I need to leave for the day," I told her. I sent an email to Sonya and Dr. Jenkins telling them that I was sick, and I left.

I can't even call Karima. She doesn't even know about me dealing with Moe. And all she'd say is, "I told you so." She was right. Moe was for the streets, and I should've never thought he would ever see me as anything more.

"Sierra, where you at?" my mother asked when I answered the phone.

"On my way home, Ma. I don't feel good. I have a headache."

More like a heartache.

"What's wrong? Did they check your pressure at work? It's probably your pressure. You don't need to be driving if it's your pressure."

"It's not my pressure, Ma. I'm almost home anyway. I just need to lie down, that's all."

"Yeah, go lie down. And make sure you drink some water. That might be why your head is hurting. You know you don't drink enough water. All you drink is coffee, and that caffeine ain't good for you. It messes with your pressure."

"I've been drinking water, Ma. But I'll drink some before I lie down." I sighed. "Did you want something?"

"Oh, yeah, I called to tell you that Reggie ain't engaged. It was just a rumor. Evelyn called and told me."

"Okay, Ma. Thanks for letting me know."

"You sure you're okay, Sierra?" she asked.

"I am, Ma. I just need to get some water and lie down," I said as I pulled in front of my condo. "I gotta go. Love you."

"Love you too."

I parked and sat in the car, unable to get out. The last person I wanted to see was Moe, who'd just stepped out of his car and was now walking toward me.

"You are a sight for sore eyes," he said and opened my door.

I ignored the hand he was holding toward me to help me, and I stepped out on my own. I closed my door and kept walking as if he weren't there.

"Sierra, what the hell?" he called out as he came up from behind.

"Leave me the hell alone, Moe, seriously," I told him.

"What? Why are you acting like this?" He had the audacity to reach for me.

I snatched away and stared at him. "Acting like what? Like someone who hasn't spoken to you in two days? Because you damn sure ain't answer my calls or call me."

"I can explain that, and I know it's fucked up, but I have had the worst forty-eight hours ever."

"I bet." I shook my head.

"First, I missed my first flight and had to fly standby, which I hate. And I lost my fucking phone in the airport. I think I threw it away accidentally, honestly. I couldn't even look for it because I had to get to my connecting flight. We sat on the tarmac for almost two hours because of some kind of mechanical issue. Got off the plane, spent the night in the airport. Then when I finally got home, I had another emergency waiting for me as soon as I pulled up to the crib that I had to take care of."

He said it so effortlessly that I almost believed him. Had I not witnessed him with Morgan with my own eyes, I probably wouldn't have ever found out. He damn sure hadn't mentioned that.

"You mean your baby mama?" I asked.

Moe's eyes popped open, and his head snapped in disbelief. He was busted, and there was no way he could get out of it.

"You must take me for a fool. You do realize the clinic you came into today was the one I work at, right? I saw the whole thing. I know you went with Morgan in the ambulance, and I know all about the miscarriage, which I am sorry about. So don't come all up in my face telling me about missing flights and losing phones. And like I said, leave me the fuck alone."

"You buggin' for real."

"Oh, I'm buggin'? Typical response—project your bullshit on me." I laughed.

"Which part is bullshit? Because I ain't projecting nothing. Morgan ain't my girlfriend or my baby mama. I've only met her twice," Moe said.

"And? It only takes once to knock someone up if you're having unprotected sex, asshole. And that chick has constantly been over here banging on your door and looking for you. I told you about her coming by banging on the door like she was the motherfuckin' police." I looked him up and down.

"She wasn't looking for me. She was looking for Ced, her baby daddy. And he's been ducking and dodging her ever since she told him she was knocked up. Her ass was sitting in the parking lot in pain and hoping I would call him for her since he wouldn't take her calls. I told her she ain't need Ced. She needed a damn doctor. So yeah, I brought her into the office, and I rode with her to the hospital because my fucked-up friend refused to man the hell up. If you saw me, why didn't you say something? I damn sure could've used some support while it was happening. But it's cool. And you just proved I was right about my first assumptions about you," he told me. "Now, per your request, I'll gladly leave you the fuck alone."

He turned and walked away, leaving me speechless as he got into his car and drove off. I wanted to run behind him, explain that I'd been wrong, and apologize. I didn't. The headache I'd lied to my mother about having was now very real. I needed some water and to lie down.

Chapter 10

I'd been waiting anxiously and listening for Moe to come back. It was almost midnight when I saw the reflection of his car lights in my bay window, then confirmed the sound of his door opening across the hall. My emotions were all over the place, even more so without having Karima to confide in. Luckily, I found a listening ear and sound advice from an unexpected source.

"Oh, Sierra, it's going to be okay. Don't cry," Sonya told me. She'd called after work to check on me and see if I needed anything, and she ended up getting a thirty-minute oral dissertation of my drama-filled love life. She wasn't judgmental or disapproving at all but her same supportive self.

"I messed up. I didn't even give him a chance to explain. I just jumped to conclusions and assumed I was being played." I sniffed. "I honestly expected him to play me."

"But why? You said the two of you enjoyed spending time and you felt like he liked you."

"I thought I was playing myself in a way. Seeing and feeling something that wasn't there. Moe is a player, and he likes a certain type of woman, and I'm nothing like it," I said. "He likes model chicks and has no problem getting them. Not girls like me. You saw him today. He's tall and handsome and successful and funny. He can have any woman he wants."

"You're a model chick, Sierra. You're beautiful, inside and out, and smart and funny and a whole lot of other

amazing qualities. Hell, you're the one who can get anyone you want. Moe ain't stupid. He knows you're a damn
good catch. Why do you think he's been with you these
past few weeks instead of those other chicks you say
are his type? He wants to be with you."

"You think so?" I asked.

"I know so. If you're not sure, then ask him. He'll tell
you. Have you even told him what you want from him or
that you like him?"

"No."

"You probably should. Why are you waiting for him
to decide? You have a choice and a say in this too. And
before you ask, if he doesn't feel the same way or he's
not sure, then that's fine too. There are plenty of tall,
handsome, successful men who will value you. Ones who
will love and accept you for exactly the size you are right
now. You ain't gotta lose a pound. My man is all of those
things and more, and he deserves all of me."

"True." I laughed.

"Talk to him, Sierra. Then go from there. The only way
you'll play yourself is if you aren't honest about your feelings," she said. "Don't worry about coming in tomorrow.
I'm giving you a mental health day, paid."

"Thanks, Sonya. I appreciate you."

After talking to her, I took out my journal and began
to write. I was honest about everything I felt. When I was
done, I remembered the dough waiting in the fridge. I
hopped up and proceeded to bake.

I waited a few minutes after he got home before finally
picking up the plate of cookies and going to see him. I
knocked on his door softly at first, then a little harder.
Finally, he opened it.

"These are for you," I told him. "They're your favorite,
chocolate chip."

He didn't respond immediately. He looked down at the plate, then back at me as he took it from my hands. "Thanks. I appreciate it."

"Can I come in?"

"Sure." He held the door open, and I stepped inside. "You want a drink?"

"No, I'm fine," I said nervously. I'd been inside his place plenty of times, but I waited for him to give me permission to sit.

"You don't have to be all formal, Sierra. You can relax," he said as he walked over to his sofa and sat down. He had a cookie in his hand and began to nibble. "These are good by the way. Or it could be that I'm hungry."

"Both," I said. "How's Morgan? You check on her?"

"She's resting. Her mom took her home. Ced's ass still hasn't called or checked on her." He shook his head.

"Karima dodged a bullet with that one," I said, recalling how he tried to push up on her at Taboo.

"This whole thing has made me reflect," he said. "I never want to be that guy."

"You're nothing like him," I said.

"I am in a lot of ways. Well, I was. Not lately though. I've changed for the better." Moe looked deep in thought. "I didn't even pick up on it until today. Losing my phone, not being able to call and tell you what was going on, I was pissed. It's crazy because the only person I wanted to talk to was you, and I couldn't. Shit was frustrating as hell."

"I know. I was scared myself and thought something had happened and you were in the hospital or hurt somewhere, and I didn't know how to find you," I told him.

"It was like a part of me was missing." Moe's eyes met mine. I saw it again, the longing that I'd seen the first time when we were together.

"I'm sorry I made the assumptions about you. I was wrong, and you didn't deserve that."

Moe reached over and took my hand. "I don't blame you. My previous behavior warranted it. I'm glad you're here with me now though."

"Moe, I need to tell you something," I said before I lost my nerve.

"What is it? Are you still in love with him?" Moe asked.

"What?"

"Your ex. You're admitting that you're still in love with him?"

"No, I'm not in love with him. Not anymore. I'm . . . I mean, I know this is gonna sound crazy, but I'm in love with you," I blurted out.

There, I said it. For the first time in my life, I'd been the one to say it first. I faced my fear of rejection and had been honest with myself and Moe.

"Wow, Sierra, I wasn't expecting that." He looked surprised. "I don't even know—"

"I get it. You don't have to say it. I'm different, and you can't see yourself with a girl like me—"

My babbling was stopped by Moe pulling me toward him and covering my mouth with his. His mouth tasted like chocolate, a result of my delicious cookies.

"Sierra," he said when we finally paused moments later.

"Yeah?" I smiled.

"You're right, I don't want to be with a girl like you. Because I'm in love with you exactly the way you are." He smiled.

My heart was overjoyed, and I couldn't believe what he'd said. I kissed him again to make sure I wasn't dreaming.

I'd gotten the man I never even knew I wanted, and I didn't have to be anyone other than who I already was.

Also available . . .

Perfectly Fine Christmas

by

La Jill Hunt

Prologue

Kendall

"Mommy, what's plump?" Kendall asked.

Her mother, who was driving, came to a stop, humming along with Stevie Wonder as he sang "That's What Christmas Means to Me," and then glanced over. "*Plump*? It means, uh . . . 'fuller.' No, wait, it means 'round.' Why?"

"Because in children's church, Mrs. Daniels was giving out parts for the pageant, and I told her I wanted to be either the star of Bethlehem or the angel, but she wouldn't let me," Kendall explained. "She said I had to be a camel."

"A what?"

"A camel," Kendall repeated. She'd been a little disappointed with the role that she'd been given, but she was still excited to be a part of the annual Christmas play with her friends.

For the past two years, she'd been a member of the children's choir, but now that she was seven, she could be a part of the best part of the play each year: the Nativity scene. She'd waited patiently as Mrs. Daniels called the names of the children who had been chosen to play Mary, Joseph, and the Three Wise Men. Those parts were assigned to the older kids, but at that moment there were still several roles available, and Kendall was excited when her name was finally called.

"Kendall Freeman, let's see what we have for you, sweetie." Mrs. Daniels peered over the brim of her glasses as she flipped through the clipboard in her hand. "You sure you don't want to be in the choir? You have such a pretty voice."

"No, ma'am." Kendall shook her head. "I wanna be in the play."

"Okay, then I think I have something that will be good for you. What about a shepherd?"

Kendall scrunched up her nose, as if she smelled something horrible. "A shepherd? No, that's for a boy, Mrs. Daniels. I don't wanna be a shepherd."

"I understand, and you're right. I don't know what I was thinking. I'm sorry. Oh, here we go." Mrs. Daniels used her pen to point to the clipboard. "Kendall Freeman, you will be this year's camel."

"But I want to be either the star or an angel," Kendall said, hoping Mrs. Daniels would scan the list of characters again.

Instead, she gave Kendall a warm smile as she placed her hand on her shoulder. "Not this year, Kendall. I don't think you'll be able to be either one of those. The costumes for the angel and the star of Bethlehem are being reused from last year, and I don't think they'll work for you."

"Why not?" Kendall whined. They reused the costumes every year; that wasn't anything new.

"Because you're a little on the plump side, and some of the other girls are a better fit. But I know that you're gonna make the best camel we've ever had, and as a matter of fact, I'm gonna talk to Miss Lauren and see if she'll even let you do the closing lines. How does that sound?"

Kendall shrugged, still not understanding why she couldn't have the part she wanted, but grateful for the consolation prize of the extra lines. She took the copy of the play that Mrs. Daniels offered her, along with the rehearsal schedule, then headed back to her seat.

"Why do you always have that doll?" Ciera, one of the girls in her age group, asked when Kendall got back to her seat.

Kendall picked up Missy, her favorite doll, and placed her in her lap. "I don't always have her. My mom won't let me take her to school, but Missy likes church, so I bring her."

"She likes church? How do you know?" Ciera looked at the doll and frowned.

"I don't know." Kendall shrugged. "I just kinda know. She's my best friend, and I like church, so she does too. Don't you and your best friend like the same things?"

Ciera's eyes went from Missy to Kendall, and then she snapped, "I don't have a best friend. And I don't have a doll, either."

"Oh." Kendall didn't know how to respond, so she just smoothed Missy's dress down and went back to listening to Mrs. Daniels call names. She noticed Ciera continuing to stare at her. She finally turned and asked, "You want to hold her?"

"Ciera McNeil," Mrs. Daniels called, and the girl hopped up and went to the front of the room. "You'll be the angel."

Ciera clapped excitedly as she jumped up and down. "Yay! That's what I wanted."

Again, Kendall was disappointed: Ciera had been given the part that she wanted. Then she looked down at Missy and felt a sense of gratitude. *At least I have you, Missy.*

By the time church ended, Kendall was hungry and ready to go. For some reason, the word *plump* still resonated in her head. As she and her mother were on the way to Sunday dinner at their favorite restaurant, Kendall decided to ask what it meant, thinking it was no big deal. She was wrong. Her mother, now visibly upset, turned the car around and drove full speed ahead back to the church.

"Stay in the car. I'll be right back," she told Kendall as she unbuckled her seat belt.

"But . . ." Kendall didn't bother saying anything else, because her mother slammed the car door and marched toward the entrance to the church. Instead, she held Missy, her favorite doll, in her arms as she looked at the stapled papers Mrs. Daniels had given her. "The Birth" was written in bold print on the top page. She was determined not to let Mrs. Daniels down, and so she vowed to be the best camel St. Joseph's Missionary Baptist Church had ever seen.

A few minutes later her mother returned to the car. "Guess what?" she said when she opened the driver's door. Kendall could see that she was still a little agitated but was smiling.

"What?" Kendall asked.

"You're not gonna be the camel," she told her. "You're gonna be the star." "Huh?"

"You're gonna be the star of Bethlehem in the pageant," her mother said matter-of-factly. "Congratulations."

"But Mrs. Daniels said—"

"Don't worry about what she said. She changed her mind. I promise you're going to be the most beautiful star of Bethlehem anyone has ever seen. But you'd better learn those lines." A huge grin spread across her mother's face as she leaned over and gave Kendall a hug. Kendall nodded excitedly. "I promise I will, Mama. I'm gonna learn all of them, and the songs too, even though I'm not in the choir."

"That's fine too," she said. "And, Kendall, don't ever let anyone tell you what you can't do. Doesn't matter if you're plump or not, you're still amazing, and you can do whatever you want to do. As long as you work hard and strive to be the best, that's all that matters."

Three weeks later, Kendall said all her lines perfectly as the star of Bethlehem and then recited the closing lines of the play. The audience gave her a standing ovation and raved at her gorgeous gold costume with the flashing lights, which her mother had crafted. Kendall was proud of herself, and from the look on her mother's face, she knew that she was proud too.

Her mother rushed over and hugged her tight after the performance was over. "You were amazing, baby! I knew you would be."

"Really, Mama? I didn't forget one word, not one." Kendall grinned.

Her mother nodded. "No, you didn't."

"Where's Missy? And Courtney?" Kendall began looking for her old doll and the new one that she'd gotten from her grandmother for Christmas. Now she had two best friends instead of one.

"They're right here." Her mother held up both dolls. "Now, grab your coat and let's get ready to go."

"But they have refreshments in the back, Mama. Can we please stay?" Kendall begged.

"Fine. For a little while. But I'm gonna need for you to take your friends and put them in the car. I'm not gonna be responsible for them, and I don't want them to get lost."

Kendall wanted Missy and Courtney to enjoy the after-party festivities, but she figured they could keep each other company for a little while in the car. She held them both tight as she followed her mother into the parking lot. "Hey, guys, you're gonna wait in the car while I get some cake, but I promise I'll be right back. Mama's gonna lock the car door, right, Ma?"

When her mother didn't respond, Kendall realized she was no longer beside her. She turned and saw that she'd walked to the corner where Cierra and her mother were waiting at the bus stop. Kendall watched as they talked for a minute. Suddenly, her mother slipped off her coat and helped Ciera's mother put it on. They hugged, and then her mother walked back over to the car.

"Mama, what did you do? Why did you give Ciera's mama your new coat? Grandma gave you that coat for Christmas," Kendall gasped.

"She did. But I didn't need a new coat, Kendall. I already have plenty of coats. Ciera's mother isn't working right now. She doesn't have a job or a coat, and I have both. It's Christmas, and God gave me the opportunity to be her angel on Earth," her mother explained.

"Angel on Earth?" Kendall frowned.

"Yeah, God blessed me so that I could bless her. That's what angels do. Remember what Ciera said in the play? She brought good tidings of great joy. That's what I just did. Showed her God's love from heaven, here on Earth. That's why we celebrate Christmas, baby." Her mother pulled her close.

Kendall looked down at the two dolls in her arms, then back over at Ciera and her mother. "I'll be right back."

"Kendall, where . . . ?"

Kendall skipped across the parking lot. When she got to Ciera, she pushed Courtney into her arms and said, "Merry Christmas."

Ciera looked shocked. She stared at the doll, then said, "Thank you."

Kendall rushed back to her mother, who welcomed her with open arms. "Kendall, sweetie, you are truly a gift. Look at you. You got to be both the star *and* an angel."

"I did, Mama. I did." Kendall nodded and smiled with joy.

Chapter 1

Kendall

The sky was dark and the usually busy street was void of both traffic and pedestrians when Kendall arrived at Diablo Designs, the high-end boutique where she'd worked as the lead seamstress for the past three years. She was grateful that the weather wasn't as cold as she'd expected it to be, considering the fact that it was five thirty in the morning. The boutique didn't open for hours. Kendall had work to do, and she was excited about getting it done before customers arrived. She carefully balanced the large brown box she had carried from the parking garage on her knee as she unlocked the back door, and then she hurried inside to disarm the security system. The store was eerily quiet, and the shadows of the mannequins throughout the open space were almost frightening. Kendall didn't waste time turning on the lights. She carried the box to the front of the store and set it down in front of the display window that held the seven-foot Christmas tree that she'd assembled two days prior.

"I can't believe we're actually doing this."

Startled, Kendall quickly turned around to see her best friend and coworker, Amber, strolling toward her. The look on her face was identical to the irritated tone of her voice.

"Good morning to you too, sunshine." Kendall smiled.

"Don't 'sunshine' me. The last thing I'm feeling right now is good, especially since it's still dark outside," Amber grumbled. "There was no sign of the sun at all."

"Well, whether the one in the sky is up or not, you will always be my sunshine, and I will always have a good morning for you when I see you. And even though you are grumpy as hell, you still look cute." Kendall beamed and put her arm around Amber's shoulders. "I like your skirt."

Amber glanced down at the denim and leather crafted skirt she wore, which happened to be custom made by Kendall. "Thanks. A friend gave it to me as a bribe to get me to come to work in the wee hours of the morning the day after Thanksgiving."

"I see it worked. Come on now, Amb. I have let you moan and groan enough. It's time for you to perk up and get into the holiday spirit, so we can get this tree decorated," Kendall told her.

"This is about as perky as I'm gonna get. You could've at least waited until after Starbucks opened." Amber sighed.

Kendall nodded. "I promise as soon as they open, I got you. You will have your venti mocha latte, with an extra shot of espresso, extra whipped cream, and a dome top. I'll even throw in an almond biscotti for you to enjoy."

Kendall knew Amber well enough to know that the gorgeous skirt wouldn't be enough to pacify her. She was willing to do whatever she had to do. There was no way she was going to be able to get everything done without a ready, willing, and able assistant. Kendall had a vision, and Amber was going to help bring it to life.

Amber folded her arms. "Oh God. Coffee and a biscotto? Something tells me you're about to be extra as hell this year."

"Not at all. I do, however, have a theme."

"You always have a theme, and it's always over the top, Kendall. Why can't we just put up a nicely decorated tree like all the other businesses on the block?"

"Because we aren't like all the other businesses, Amber. We are Diablo Designs, home of the couture maestro herself, Deena Diablo. We don't do *nice*. We do exquisite. This year we will be displaying a winter wonderland. Snow, icicles, snowflakes, and plenty of bling."

"Fine. What do you wanna do first?" Amber groaned.

"Come on, Am. You already know." Kendall smiled.

"God, no, Kendall. It's too early." Amber's head moved back and forth.

"It's the only way to start." Kendall shrugged as she backed up toward the sales counter. She reached under it and opened the cabinet where the sound system was located, then connected it to her phone's Bluetooth. Seconds later the store was filled with the sound of Chris Brown crooning the lyrics to her all-time favorite Christmas song, "This Christmas." Kendall danced her way back across the store and forced a reluctant Amber to sing and sway along. By the time the song had ended and the next one had begun playing, the two of them were excitedly opening the huge box containing lights, garland, and Kendall's beloved Christmas ornaments. The decorating had begun.

Two hours later, as they were finishing up, Deena, Kendall and Amber's boss, walked into the showroom and stopped in her tracks. "Wow! It's beautiful," she exclaimed as she gazed at the tree. She was wearing a gorgeous black tuxedo-style pantsuit that fit her perfectly. With her height of almost six feet, her slender frame, and her high cheekbones, Deena could easily be a model for the designs she created. Everything about her exuded elegance, and it was apparent even in the way she stood back and gracefully waved her hands toward the display they were in the midst of completing.

Kendall, who was in the middle of draping ivory cloth along the bottom of the raised display area, stood up. "You like it?" she asked.

"I love it, Kendall. Every year I tell you that you've outdone yourself, but this year you truly have. I mean, the tree is gorgeous, but this entire space looks like a . . ."

"Winter wonderland," Kendall and Amber said simultaneously.

"Yes, that's exactly what it is." Deena clapped. "And you two managed to get all of this done before it's time to open. That's incredible."

"We had fun doing it." Kendall nodded with excitement. "It didn't even feel like work, really."

Amber raised an eyebrow. "Yeah, it was a blast. You should've come and helped."

Deena laughed, and her caramel complexion made the red lipstick she wore seem even brighter. "Looks like you two had everything under control. You didn't need my help. Besides, with everything I'm responsible for around here, do you think I have time to have fun?"

Kendall gave a warning look just before her friend was about to make another comment, and Amber went back to hanging lights. Although they both loved their jobs, they had a difference of opinion when it came to their boss. Kendall, who worked as a seamstress in the boutique, adored Deena and appreciated the mentorship she provided. Amber, the boutique's top sales consultant, admired and respected Deena, but she felt that her boss was quite self-serving and micro-aggressive and insensitive at times. Kendall often reminded her that because Deena was one of the most sought-after designers of formal couture, her job kept her so busy that she didn't realize what she said most of the time, and she meant nothing by her comments. Over the years, Kendall had become accustomed to Deena's demeanor a little more than Amber had. The reason for this was that in addition to being her boss, Deena had also been one of her mother's friends.

Deena put her arm around Kendall's shoulders, and they stared at the majestic tree, which was now covered in sparkling crystals, white ornaments, and clear lights. "It's beautiful, Kendall. Actually, it's absolutely stunning."

"Not yet." Kendall shook her head. "Almost, but it's missing one thing."

Within seconds, Amber walked over and placed a glossy stained wooden box in Kendall's hands. Kendall tried not to tremble as she opened it. Inside, buried under soft white satin, was one of her most prized possessions: the tree-topper figurine, an angel, that had been passed down for three generations in her family. She carefully lifted it out of the box and smiled in an effort to avoid tears.

Get it together, Kendall. It's the season of joy, not sorrow.

After she adjusted the wings and the fur-trimmed coat of the precious brown porcelain figurine, Kendall held it out. "Here," she said to Deena. "You do the honors."

"Oh, Kendall, no. You do it. It was her favorite part," Deena replied, sounding as if she was just as close to crying as Kendall.

Kendall nodded. "I know. That's why you should do it."

Deena carefully cradled the angel in her hands, and then she stepped up the ladder beside the tree. She positioned the angel atop the tree so that it was upright and secure, then eased back down the ladder. Then the three women stood back and marveled, taking in the end results of the labor that Kendall and Amber had put in for the past few hours. The tree, in Kendall's eyes, was perfect.

"The angel has been placed atop the Christmas tree. We know what that means," Deena whispered.

"Time for the magic to begin." Amber smiled.

Kendall nodded. "Exactly."

"I wonder what Aunt Nichole is going to task us with this year," Amber mused, staring at the tree topper.

Kendall shrugged. "I don't know, but I'm sure we'll soon find out." Without fail, every year since her death, Nichole's mother, it seemed, sent each of them what they'd come to call "angel assignments." These assignments weren't as simple as serving meals at the local shelter or organizing the successful toy drive they held each year in the boutique. No, they usually involved unusual circumstances that seemed to come out of nowhere. For instance, one year Deena paid the hotel bill for a traveling family of four whose car had broken down in front of the store. Another year Amber treated one of their clients' entire fourth grade class to a presentation of *The Nutcracker* after the funding from the school fell through. Kendall lost count of how many times she had paid tabs at restaurants or grocery stores because someone didn't have enough money.

"She's right." Deena laughed. "We never have to wait too long once the angel is in place. That thing is like a bat signal for the Christmas holidays." Deena's tone went from pleasant to direct as she shifted gears. "We need to get in place for the busy day ahead, and the two of you need to get changed. Doors open in fifteen minutes. I hope there's a cup of coffee waiting for me, since you two have some."

Kendall glanced at the two cups of Starbucks that she had had delivered as soon as the app allowed her to order. "Of course. Yours is waiting for you in your office."

Deena smiled. "Good. I can't be upset about your drinking coffee on the showroom floor if I'm doing the same, right?" She walked away, then suddenly stopped and turned back. "Great job on the display, ladies, but let's get these leftover decorations put away and let's play more fitting music," she added. "The holiday songs are fine, but find something a little less urban. Staff meeting in ten minutes, so get to it."

"I swear, I love that woman, but she gets on my nerves," Amber hissed when Deena was out of earshot. "She should've been the one bringing coffee to us, instead of asking if there was some for her. And what the heck does 'less urban' mean? Since when are the Jackson 5 considered urban? Has she forgotten that she's black too?"

"Deena knows that, Amber. The problem is she's bourgeois," Kendall said as they packed up the remaining Christmas decorations. "She also looks at how everything will affect her bottom line. Look at the caliber of our clientele. They're just as *siddity* as she is, and so is everyone else who works here. You and I are the only cool kids."

"You stay defending her, but I get it." Amber sighed and picked up the box with the decorations. "I hope when you start your own fashion line, you don't become 'less urban' and you keep it real, meaning black."

"Girl, you are hilarious, and you know my starting my own line ain't happening anytime soon. I keep telling you that I'm not even close to being ready," Kendall commented as she picked up the two now empty coffee cups.

"As far as I can see, you are ready. Your designs are incredible. The same people who pay Deena top dollar will pay you," Amber continued, as if they hadn't had this conversation dozens of times already. "You and I both know people are trying to get you to make stuff now."

Kendall could admit that she did have amazing design ideas, and her sewing skills were impeccable. But starting a designer clothing line would take a lot more than artwork and a sewing machine. She knew her dream would happen one day. Until that time came, she was grateful to have a job in her field and to work for a high-end designer who paid her well and gave her the opportunity to do what she loved. And despite the fact that she had been approached about sewing projects outside the boutique, the noncompete agreement Deena had required her to sign prevented her from doing so.

"I love the way you believe in me, Am. That's why you're my bestie. I promise, when I start my own label, I'll charge you only half of the retail cost for the garments." Kendall nudged her and pointed to Amber's skirt. "Now, hurry up, so we can change out of this 'urban attire' and get back out there for Insight."

After they had cleaned up from the morning activities and had changed into their work attire, Kendall and Amber rushed back onto the floor so they wouldn't miss the morning meeting, which Deena referred to as "Insight." Like their boss, the entire staff wore all black. It was a requirement for everyone. Although Kendall spent most of the day in the alterations room, she was still expected to observe the rule, because there were times when she was called to assist clients. She didn't mind the dress code. Black wasn't her favorite color choice, but it was easy to put together black pieces. Plus, the color was slimming. Not that she felt the need to look thinner.

Kendall was quite comfortable in her curvaceous, size twenty, larger-than-average body, despite being the only plus-size employee at Diablo Designs. Her wide hips, ample DDD breasts, thick waist, and vivacious derriere worked to her advantage. Because nothing at Diablo's went beyond a size twelve, Kendall was exempt from having to wear certain signature pieces, the cost of which would have been deducted from her paycheck. Amber, who wore a size ten, wasn't so lucky.

Deena smiled at all the staff members gathered around. "I hope you all had a fantastic Thanksgiving, are well rested and recharged for today. Special thanks to Kendall and Amber for the beautiful window display to welcome our clients and get them in the spirit to buy gifts." Deena gazed at each of her employees. "In addition to fulfilling the seasonal needs of our regular customers and Christmas brides, the holidays also mean the start of something else, right?"

They all nodded and shouted in unison, "Holiday ball season!"

Chapter 2

Niya

"Niya, please sit up and put that away. The dining-room table is no place for a cell phone."

Niya quickly slid her cell phone into her pocket and sat straight in her chair without even looking at her grandmother, who'd given her the instructions. Instead, she focused on her food, picking at the rubbery turkey bacon beside the eggs and toast. She didn't mind the eggs but would've preferred regular bacon and some jelly on the dry bread instead of the pat of margarine. Deciding to make the best of her breakfast situation, Niya placed the meat and eggs on the toast and was in the process of folding it when once again, she was scolded.

"That is not the proper way to eat. I didn't prepare a plate for you to eat a poorly constructed sandwich like it came from a cheap fast-food drive-through. Why would you do that?" her grandmother said.

Again, Niya quickly straightened up. She dropped her sandwich onto her plate and stared at it. At this point, it was as if she couldn't do anything right, not even eat breakfast. Grandma Claudia constantly picked at every little thing. Niya didn't make her bed properly, because the sheet wasn't ever tucked in tight enough. Her clothes weren't hung up correctly, because the hangers should all be facing the same direction. Not that this should have mattered, considering the fact that she had commented that Niya's clothes were unappealing.

What does that even mean? Who am I supposed to appeal to in a T-shirt, jeans, and sneakers? Niya had wondered at the time.

Being at her grandmother's house was exhausting, tiresome, and lonely. She missed her mom. It had been two weeks since the car accident that had robbed Niya of the one person who loved her no matter how she looked or the manner in which she chose to eat her breakfast. The last fourteen days felt like a continual, endless nightmare, and it all started when Mrs. Hester, the guidance counselor at her school, had come and got her out of her AP English class and had escorted her to the main office. Mrs. Hester, who was usually full of chatter, had been oddly silent. Something about her energy had seemed off.

"Am I in trouble?" Niya had asked as they walked down the vacant hallway. She knew that she wasn't, considering the fact that other than to her two best friends, she barely talked to anyone in school.

"No, sweetheart." Mrs. Hester put her arm around Niya's shoulder. "Not at all."

"Is this about the field trip to the planetarium?" Niya asked. "I told Mr. Hawkins that I'd rather do a written assignment instead of going. I've been to the planetarium, like, four times since third grade, and I really think it would be a pointless trip," she explained. She also dreaded the thought of being on a crowded school bus with her rambunctious classmates for forty-five minutes, riding to a place where the only thing most of them planned on doing was fool around in the darkness instead of learning about constellations. Granted, Niya had no desire to learn about the stars, either, but she definitely wasn't interested in getting groped by any of her classmates.

"This isn't about the field trip." Mrs. Hester sighed.

Niya's anxiety increased when they arrived at the main office. As soon as she entered the glass-encased area, everyone immediately stopped what they were doing and stared.

"Niya, sweetie."

Niya was so focused on the stares that she didn't even realize Ms. Monica, her best friend Jada's mom, was there and had spoken to her until she was pulled into a tight hug.

"Miss Monica, what are you doing here? Where's Jada?" Niya frowned, noticing the tears in Miss Monica's eyes.

"Jada's in class," Mrs. Hester told Niya. "Come into my office, so we can talk." Mrs. Hester guided them past the administrative area, into the guidance counselor's suite, and then into her private office. S he sat down at her desk, and Miss Monica took one of the chairs on the other side. "Sit down, Niya."

Niya sat, now afraid about what was happening. "Is something wrong with Jada? Is she sick?"

"No, baby, Jada's not sick," Miss Monica assured her as she shook her head and placed her hand on Niya's arm. Niya noticed her glance at Mrs. Hester before she continued. "Jada's fine. But we need to tell you something."

"What? What is it? You're scaring me, Miss Monica." Niya's heart raced even faster as she looked her in the eyes.

Miss Monica took a deep breath but became choked up when she tried to speak. Mrs. Hester walked over, gave her a tissue, and then knelt beside Niya. In that moment, Niya knew why she'd been brought to the office, why Miss Monica was there, and why everyone had been staring at her.

"My mom?" Niya whispered.

Mrs. Hester nodded. "Yes. There was an accident."

Niya's breathing was so hard that she saw the rise and fall of her own chest. "Accident? Where is she? Is she okay? Can you take me to her, Miss Monica?"

"Baby, she . . . she . . . is . . ." Miss Monica choked up again.

Niya jumped from her seat, nearly knocking down Mrs. Hester. "I have to get to her."

Mrs. Hester shook her head. "Niya. She's gone."

Niya's body began to shake. "You're lying," she responded, her voice trembling.

It can't be true. Somebody has made a mistake. My mom is at work. She's picking me up from Jada's house, and we're going to the Chinese buffet, like we do every Thursday night. Afterward, we're heading home and getting there just in time to curl up on the couch, under her favorite blanket, and watch Grey's Anatomy.

Ms. Monica stood and put her arms around Niya. "I'm so sorry. It's gonna be okay."

"We're here for you, Niya." Mrs. Hester rubbed her back.

"Don't." Niya quickly moved away from both of them. The last thing she wanted was to be touched, comforted, or held. She wanted her mother.

Niya would quickly learn that wanting and having were two very different things. There was nothing she could do to have her mother ever again. Before she could process that nightmare, a funeral was held, the casket holding her mother's body was lowered into the grave, and Niya was packed up and moved in with her grandmother, whom she barely knew.

"May I be excused?" Niya said now, her voice barely above a whisper. Niya didn't understand the purpose of asking permission to leave the table once she had finished with her meal. The whole thing seemed cold and formal, much like her new home and its owner.

Her grandmother looked at her, then tilted her head. "You're finished?"

Niya nodded. "Yes, ma'am."

"Yes, you may," Grandma Claudia said with a brief nod.

Niya slid her chair back, stood, and quickly reached for her plate, which held the same amount of food as when she had sat down. The only difference was the toast, which was now bent from the makeshift sandwich that hadn't made it to her mouth.

"We have plans this morning. I expect you to be ready to leave in thirty minutes," her grandmother declared.

"Plans?" Niya paused.

"Yes. I have some shopping to do, and you need to get out of the house. You haven't been out since your arrival. It will be good for you," her grandmother told her. "Besides, the Christmas preparations for the house will start today, and the noise will be unbearable."

She's gotta be kidding. No way. I'm not going anywhere with her, Niya thought.

Just as she was about to voice her objection, Niya heard movements coming from the hallway, then the opening of the front door. She didn't say another word as she walked out of the dining room. She went into the kitchen, scraped her food into the garbage, then shoved the plate into the dishwasher. Niya tried her best not to make any excess noise or bring any attention to herself as she hustled out the back door. She prayed, *Please don't be gone. Please don't be gone.*

"Uncle Reese!" she called out as she rounded the side of the house. When she spotted the sleek motorcycle heading down the driveway, her heart raced and she stopped, knowing there was no way she could chase him and catch up once he pulled out of the driveway. She was already out of breath. The all too familiar feeling of a knot forming in her throat caught her attention, and she tried to swallow it down, knowing that tears would soon follow. As she watched the wheels of the bike roll, her heart sank.

It's too late.

Suddenly, just as he got to the end of the driveway, instead of pulling off, he stopped the bike. It was as if Uncle Reese had sensed her watching. He planted his feet on the pavement, then turned his torso and looked in her direction. Niya quickly waved and ran at record speed across the yard.

"I thought I heard someone calling me," he said when she reached his side. He smiled, turned off the engine, and flipped the eye cover of his helmet up so he could look at her.

"Where are you going?" Niya asked.

"I need to go into work, grab my schedule, and talk to my boss. You know I go back to work Monday, so I gotta make sure everything's straight," Uncle Reese said.

"Can't you do that later? Do you have to go now?" Niya's voice cracked.

"Yeah, I gotta go take care of it now. What's wrong?" He frowned. "You all right? Did something happen?"

"Not really, but . . ." Niya shrugged instead of completing her sentence. Yes, something happened, Uncle Reese. My mother died! she thought. She wanted to remind him of this in case he had forgotten.

"Niya, what's going on?" Uncle Reese placed his hands on her shoulders and looked her in the eyes.

"Grandma Claudia, she . . ." Niya shrugged again.

Uncle Reese removed his helmet and groaned. "Oh God. What did she do now? Just tell me."

"She says that I've been "cooped up" inside, and she's making me go shopping and run errands with her," Niya announced. "I don't want to go, Uncle Reese. Please stay so I can hang here with you," she pleaded.

Uncle Reese gave her a sympathetic smile. "Listen, I get it, and I understand why you don't wanna go. But I can't save you on this one."

"Please, Uncle Reese. I can't deal." Niya shook her head.

"Yes, you can." Uncle Reese nodded. "She's right about your needing to get out of the house. It's time. We've all gotta get back to . . . normal."

Normal? How? Nothing about my life is normal anymore.

Again, she wondered if Uncle Reese had forgotten that she was grieving the loss of her mother. And she now lived in a strange house, one that she didn't feel like leaving just yet.

"I'm not ready," Niya whispered and then looked down at the ground so Uncle Reese couldn't see the tears that threatened to fall from her eyes.

"Yes, you can. You're gonna be fine. I promise. Getting out, even though you'll be with her, is good for you. You have to leave the house, anyway, on Monday, right?" He raised an eyebrow at her.

"Don't remind me." Niya shook her head. The thought of going to school on Monday gave her as much anxiety as the idea of running errands with her grandmother. She didn't want to do either one.

"Trust me, I know my mother. She won't be out for long. Especially with them here." He motioned toward the front of the house.

Niya turned to see two vans and a large delivery truck with the name Carmichael's Nursery on the side. A couple of men were adjusting ladders against the house, while others were unloading plastic buckets.

"What are they doing?" Niya asked.

"Decorating. Who do you think makes this place look like it belongs on the Strip in Vegas?" Uncle Reese laughed.

"They're the ones who hang the lights?" Niya asked, watching a young guy who looked her age carrying a box with silver tinsel hanging out of the top. In the past Niya and her mother had visited her grandmother's home only once a year: on Christmas Day. Each year, as they drove away, Niya would turn around and stare at the family mansion, lit up like a gigantic gingerbread house. All the other homes in the neighborhood had Christmas lights as well, but the Fine mansion, which sat at the back of the cul-de-sac and also happened to be the largest, was the brightest of them all. People would come for miles just to see it. "

What? Did you think your grandma climbed up there and decorated it herself ?" Uncle Reese laughed.

"I never thought about it, honestly," Niya mumbled.

"Well, I gotta get outa here, kiddo." He went to put the helmet back on. "Have fun with Grandma."

Niya glared at him. "Not funny, Uncle Reese."

"I'm just trying to make you smile, Niya-Boo. You know you're my favorite niece."

"I'm your *only* niece, Uncle Reese." Niya gave him a blank stare. "Will you be here when we come back home?"

Instead of answering her question, Uncle Reese looked away for a second, then back at her. His lack of a verbal response made Niya uneasy.

"Oh my God! You're not coming back?" Niya gasped.

"Niya, I haven't been to my condo in weeks," he said.

"But you promised . . . ," Niya whined.

"I promised I'd stay here with you until you got settled. You knew it wasn't permanent. Don't act like that," Uncle Reese said as Niya folded her arms and turned to walk away.

"How am I supposed to act? I wish someone would please tell me. According to you, I'm wrong for being upset right now, and we both know how *she* feels. I don't eat right, dress right, breathe right. Why did she bring me here in the first place? I could've stayed with my friend Jada and her family. At least they wanted me." Niya's bottom lip quivered as she brushed away the tears.

Uncle Reese climbed off his bike, walked over to Niya, and gathered her in his arms. His presence was the only reason Niya was able to tolerate being in the house. She knew his being there was only temporary, but she hadn't expected him to leave so soon. She was less lonely with him there. It was like having a friend in the house. They laughed and talked, hung out and watched TV. They were there for each other, because truth be told, neither of them was comfortable around her grandmother. Grandma Claudia seemed to be as dissatisfied with him as she was with Niya. If Uncle Reese cared about that, he certainly didn't show it. He acted as if Grandma Claudia's constant comments about him were entertainment rather than criticism.

"Niya, we are your family, and we love you." His voice was tender.

"You tolerate me. That's not love. My mother loved me. Jada and her mom love me." Niya sniffled. "They told both of you that I could stay with them. They wanted me at their home."

"You're my niece, my sister's only child. Here is the only place I want you to be."

"You don't, and neither does she. But it's cool. At least you can leave. I'm stuck living here with someone who isn't kind to me. She doesn't even like me. She treats me like a guest, not family. The only time she talks to me is while we're eating, and then it's to correct something I've done wrong," Niya told him.

"Grandma Claudia just has an odd way of showing her love, that's all. She can be uptight and frigid, but her intentions are in the right place. She just has a funny way of showing it, that's all. Believe me, she does," he said. "You'll grow to see it."

"Niya! What are you doing out here?" Grandma Claudia's voice caused both of them to turn around. "You should be getting dressed. I told you we have places to go."

"She was saying goodbye to me, that's all," Uncle Reese yelled back. "She's coming in now."

Grandma Claudia folded her arms and shook her head, then began talking to the men working on the house. "Please be careful not to mess up my flower beds. Move that ladder over to the left. I don't want it to disrupt the bushes."

"Yes, Mrs. Fine," one of the men answered and obliged.

"Niya! Now!" Grandma Claudia yelled before returning inside.

Niya glanced at her uncle and said, "Bye, Uncle Reese."

"Hey, I love you. It's gonna be okay. Who knows? You may actually have fun." He gave her a weak smile.

"I doubt it." Niya turned and stepped away.

"I tell you what. How about we swap promises? If you'll promise to at least try to have a good time, then I promise to order pizza for dinner tonight." Uncle Reese grinned.

Niya rushed over to her uncle and gave him a hug. "Deal."

Chapter 3

Reese

"Well, well, well, look who decided to show up for a shift. Vacation over," Herb yelled as Reese walked into the ambulance bay of the rescue station. Rick and Emmi, two other coworkers, appeared on the other side of the ambulance.

"Wow. Vacation?" Reese responded to Herb's dry humor.

"Don't be a jerk, Herb," Emmi scolded before she approached Reese and gave him a hug. "How are you? Good to see you back."

"I'm good, Em. Just checking in today. I'll be back in full swing on Monday, though," Reese said.

"That's good, man. You were definitely missed." Rick shook Reese's hand. "Everything cool with your family?"

"Come on now. You know the answer to that question." Reese gave Rick, his best friend since elementary school and now his roommate, a knowing look.

"Ah, man, you know what I mean." Rick shrugged. "Maybe that wasn't the right choice of words."

"How's Niya?" Emmi asked. "Is she adjusting?"

"It's hard to say, honestly. Niya's always been a quiet kid. She hasn't really said much, other than the fact that she'd rather be living with her best friend's family than with my mother," Reese explained.

"Can't say I blame her," Rick said. "Your mom is kind of . . . abrasive."

"Exactly. Nina was definitely more of a nurturer. Although my mom means well, that's not who she is. I think that's why my sister didn't bring Niya around a lot." Reese sighed.

"Let's not forget that your mom hated Niya's dad before he passed away," Herb volunteered. "That probably had a lot to do with it as well."

They all turned and stared at him.

Emmi's head moved back and forth. "That really didn't need to be said, Herb. Please, go finish taking inventory."

"I'm just saying." Herb shrugged and then scurried back to what he was doing.

"There's a lot going on, and I feel bad for Niya," Reese told them. "She thinks we don't realize everything she's dealing with. And that's not the case."

"At least she has you, though, bro." Rick patted him on the shoulder.

"Yes, and you guys have a great relationship," Emmi offered.

"True, but as much as I love Niya, I *cannot* move into that house. I've been staying there since the funeral, but now it's time for me to get back to work and into my own space," Reese continued. "My plan was for that to happen today, but she damn near had a meltdown before I left the house."

"Aw, poor baby. You've gotta give her some time." Emmi sighed.

"Yeah, I know, which is why I promised to go back tonight, even though I have a date. Someone isn't gonna be happy when I cancel it." Reese didn't miss the slight eye roll Emmi gave him. "What?"

"If someone doesn't understand the need for you to spend time with your niece, then that's their problem, not yours," Emmi commented.

"I didn't say Lynnette wouldn't understand, Em. I said she won't be too happy," Reese responded.

"Now you know how Emmi is. The last thing she wants to hear about is another woman," Rick teased. "Her jealous streak is showing."

As soon as Rick made the joke, Reese knew it wasn't going to be received as funny. Emmi never hid the fact that she didn't like who Reese was dating. She had no romantic interest in Reese. Her response was a result of their brother-sister-like relationship; she didn't feel as if any woman he selected was good enough. Emmi found flaws in one way or another.

"Me? Jealous? Of who? Not *her*. Believe me, there is no reason for it, sweetie," Emmi snapped at Reese.

Reese held his hands up, as if he was surrendering. "Why you yelling at me?"

Rick shrugged. "Look, I gotta agree with Em on this one, Reese. Niya needs you right now. She's the priority. Your girl ain't gonna like it, but it is what it is. You already know the crib ain't going nowhere. Just give a brother a heads-up before you come home."

"Why do I need to give you notice before I come to the spot I pay for each month?" Reese asked.

It had been over a week since he'd stopped by the condo they shared to pick up his mail and more clothes. The place hadn't been as clean as it usually was when he was there, but nothing had seemed too out of sorts. Rick was known to throw a party not only without giving a reason but also without consulting Reese beforehand. Reese was sure he'd been enjoying having the place to himself.

"I just wanna make sure it's in tip-top shape, that's all. You know how upset you get when there's a bowl and spoon in the sink," Rick teased.

"Just make sure the dishes are washed every day and you won't have to worry about when I come back," Reese told him.

"Fine! Is this a social call, or are you here to check in?" Captain Yates yelled from the doorway of the station.

Reese waved at him. "I was just on my way to see you, sir."

"Then come on in and let these folks get back to what they are supposed to be doing," Captain Yates barked. "Herb seems to be the only one working."

They all turned and looked at Herb, who was now suddenly hard at work, with a clipboard in hand, instead of leaning against the rig, eavesdropping on their conversation.

"Yes, sir," Reese said. "A'ight, y'all, we'll catch up later. Emmi, as always, thanks for the advice. Rick, wash those damn dishes and replace my juice."

Reese hugged both of them before going inside. He missed his work family, even Herb. They had been truly supportive of him after the loss of his sister. Captain Yates had checked on him just as much as Emmi and Rick, and he'd made the three-hour drive to attend Nina's funeral. His boss's presence there had spoken volumes. Working together the past seven years had made them a tight-knit group. The long shifts, the small shared living and working quarters, and just the level of teamwork their job required had resulted in the special bond.

Captain Yates nodded when Reese entered his office. "Good to see you, Fine. Everything all right with your family?"

"For the most part. My niece is getting settled, and my mother seems to be getting back into her routine." Reese sat in the chair closest to the door.

"And what about you? How are you feeling?" The captain looked him in the eye.

"I'm good. Ready to come back and do my thing." Reese shrugged. "I've missed it."

"Understood, and we're anticipating your return. I just want to make sure you're ready," Captain Yates said.

"I am. I've been keeping up with my working out and running daily—"

"That's not what I'm talking about, Fine. Your physical fitness has never been a problem. I'm more concerned about your suffering a traumatic loss, a major one. I don't want you to feel like you have to rush back. This job is just as much mental as it is physical."

Reese nodded. "I know, Captain. I assure you, I'm ready."

"All right. We'll see you on Monday, at six a.m.," Captain Yates said. "That's where we'll keep you until the New Year."

Reese frowned. "Morning shift? That's it? Captain, I can go back to my regular schedule."

"Let's see how it goes. Trust me on this one, Fine."

Reese had no choice but to trust Captain Yates, who'd been his supervisor for six of the seven years he'd been at the rescue station. Reese had been hired and had started as an EMT. Now he was a paramedic who held the position of sergeant, thanks to Captain Yates's mentorship. As much as Reese looked forward to getting back in his regular routine of working nonstop, he knew his boss was not going to allow it, despite it being the busiest season of the year.

"First shift it is," Reese agreed. "I'll be here bright and early."

"See you Monday, Fine," Captain Yates told him as they shook hands before Reese exited the office.

After saying his goodbyes to Emmi, Rick, and the rest of the crew, Reese was about to place his helmet on his head and climb back on his motorcycle when a sleek silver Lexus pulled up and parked directly in front of him. He watched with a smile as Lynnette Graham, the sexy driver, stepped out. It had been a few days since he'd seen her. As she walked toward him, he took in the small, beautiful woman headed in his direction.

"Let me find out you're stalking me," Reese said.

"I mean, at this point that seems like the only way I'm going to see you." Lynnette's sarcastic response didn't surprise him. She'd been quite vocal about her dissatisfaction with his recent lack of attention.

"Aw, don't be like that." Reese reached out, took her arm, and pulled her to him, then rested his hands on her slender hips. The soft scent of Rose Prick, her favorite Tom Ford perfume, drifted into his nostrils.

Lynnette wrapped her arms around his neck and stared at him with her beautiful brown eyes. "Would you prefer that I not miss you, Reese?"

"Of course I want you to miss me. I miss you too, Lynnette," he told her.

"Good. I hope you are ready to show me just how much later on tonight, after dinner, because I am ready." She seductively licked her lips.

Reese didn't respond immediately, because he was trying to think of the right words to say so that Lynnette wouldn't be too reactive. Lynnette must have interpreted his pause as an indication of what he was preparing to say, because she spoke before he did.

"You can't be serious. Again, Reese?" she snapped as her arms dropped to her sides. She tried to turn and walk off, but his tightened grip prevented her from moving.

"I know, but listen, Niya is still a little uncomfortable at the house without me being there."

"That's why you need to leave." Lynnette sighed. "I'm not trying to sound mean, but if you allow her to start guilt-tripping you into staying and you're always there, she'll never adjust. She's gonna have to just deal with it."

Reese understood what Lynnette was saying, as well as the frustration she felt. They hadn't been intimate in a while. He was certain that she needed some bedroom time just as much as he did. The idea of one of their marathon sessions crossed his mind. As much as he wanted to spend time with Lynnette, it would have to wait. His priority right now was Niya and her well-being.

"Trust me, I'm just as frustrated as you are. But I'm not going to abandon my niece. She's mourning and adjusting. It's gonna take a little while longer," Reese responded, attempting to be diplomatic about the situation.

"How much longer, Reese?"

"Not much, I promise. And we can definitely go to dinner tomorrow night. That I can do. We can go to Tampico's." Reese's arms encircled her, and he gave her a pleading look. Thinking the invitation to her favorite restaurant wouldn't be enough, he decided to sweeten the deal. "Maybe we can hit up a couple of your fave designer stores before we go eat."

Lynnette didn't respond immediately, but the tightness of her lips softened, and her eyebrows, which had been raised, slowly lowered. Both were positive signs.

"I wanna spend time with you, Lynn. I miss you. You know that." Reese pulled her closer.

"And what about Niya?"

"What about her?"

"Won't she be *scared* at the house with your mother?"

The way Lynnette asked the question, Reese couldn't tell if she was being sarcastic or concerned.

"Scared?" he repeated to impel her to clarify exactly what she meant.

"I mean, isn't that why you said you have to stay there? Because she doesn't want to be alone with your mother?" Lynnette's eyebrows went back to their raised position.

"Not scared. Uncomfortable. My mother isn't the most welcoming person in the world. It's more than just that. Like I said, she's been through a lot. But we'll be out only a few hours, and she'll be fine." Reese sighed.

"Well, dinner and shopping are cool with me, I guess. But I'm not trying to be on a time limit. I'm a grown-ass woman. I don't have a curfew, so if that's gonna be a problem—"

Reese cut Lynnette's words off by covering her mouth with his. The kiss was enough to halt her complaint, but the familiar rise of Reese's nature signaled that if he didn't stop now, he would quickly arrive at the point of no return. The way Lynnette's hands were rubbing his back, and the way she was moaning lightly, indicated that she wasn't far from getting there herself. Reese pressed his forehead against hers.

"Dinner tomorrow?" he whispered.

Lynnette, still breathless, nodded.

After placing his helmet on his head, Reese climbed back on his bike and drove off. He smiled at the thought of Lynnette still standing there, with a satisfied smile on her face.

She tries to play hard core, but I know exactly how to get her to melt.

Chapter 4

Kendall

"Kendall, you've done it again. It's perfect," Mrs. Tucker said as she admired herself in the mirror. The silver gown, which had seemed two sizes too big at the top and a size too small in the hips when she purchased it two weeks ago, now fit like a glove.

Instead of suggesting another dress, Deena had assured Mrs. Tucker that if she paid the hefty price on the tag, Kendall would make the minor adjustments and simple alterations needed, and the gown would be ready in days. Despite there having been nothing minor or simple about the total reconstruction of the gown, Kendall had worked her magic, and it had resulted in the smile on Mrs. Tucker's face.

"It looks amazing," Amber said as she admired Kendall's handiwork from the doorway.

"I can't wait for them to announce Simon and me at the ball." Mrs. Tucker turned and looked at Amber. "You're sure no one else has this gown, right? You double-checked?"

Amber nodded. "I did. You will be the only one at the Rotary Holiday Ball in this design. I triple checked." One of the reasons their clients preferred shopping at Diablo's Designs was that in addition to the exclusivity of Deena's label, they were assured that they would not arrive at prestigious balls wearing the same dress. Each dress was catalogued according to the ball where it would be worn to avoid such a situation happening.

"Good. I can imagine the reaction people are going to have when they see me in this. I'm so much smaller than last year, you know?" Mrs. Tucker smoothed her hands along the metallic-sequined fabric hugging her body.

Kendall nodded and said, "You are definitely a different size than last year. I'll bag it up and bring it to the front for you."

"Thank you again, Kendall," Mrs. Tucker said as she slipped out of the gown.

After carefully collecting the fabric in her arms, Kendall carried the gown back into the alterations room and placed it on one of the custom satin hangers with the Diablo Designs logo. She admired her work one final time before she placed it in one of their signature bags.

Another one done, she thought, then turned around and saw the racks of gowns that remained. Deena was right: ball season was in full effect. The number of orders seemed endless, between dresses for holiday events and the debutante balls. Instead of being overwhelmed by the amount of work that needed to be done within the next few weeks, Kendall was excited. She loved the balls, and even though she hadn't attended one in years, being a part of the preparation brought her a sense of contentment.

There was nothing like looking at the pictures posted on social media of ladies all glammed up in the Deena Diablo dresses that she had helped create. Ball season also gave her another reason to love Christmas. In addition to the already high holiday spirits, the anticipation and excitement of the balls brought even more energy to the already busy boutique. And even though she had plenty of alteration work, it was the one time of year when she spent time on the showroom floor with everyone else.

"All bagged up and ready to go," Kendall said as she delivered Mrs. Tucker's gown to the register. She paused and looked around the crowded store. "Where's Mrs. Tucker?"

"To the left, to the left." Her coworker Luigi motioned with his hand as he rang up a woman who seemed to be so mesmerized by his black, shoulder-length, curly hair, dark olive skin, and perfect teeth that she didn't even realize he was waiting for her to insert her credit card into the machine. "I think she's looking at another gown for the First Noel."

"What? Why?" Kendall frowned. "She has already bought three gowns, two of which I still have to alter."

"I know. But based on how she has Amber cornered over there near the new arrivals rack, it looks like she'll be getting a fourth." Luigi shrugged as he stretched his already long neck to get a better look at what he was reporting.

"Amber won't let that happen." Kendall shook her head, confident that her best friend would tell Mrs. Tucker that buying another gown would be pointless, because there wouldn't be time for the proper alterations.

"She won't be able to do that, but Deena might," Luigi smirked. "She's headed over there now."

Kendall hung the bag on the rack behind the register and hastily made her way across the store. Any other time, she wouldn't be concerned, but Deena had been known to make special allowances for high-paying clients like Mrs. Tucker and to overpromise in an effort to make the sale. Kendall needed to make sure that didn't happen today.

Deena smiled as Kendall walked up. "We were just talking about you."

"Oh really?" Forcing a pleasant smile on her face to mask her concern, Kendall waited to hear what had been said instead of reacting too quickly.

"Yes, I told Deena that my gown fits so perfectly that it almost looks like a brand-new design." Mrs. Tucker smiled. "Deena, this young lady is somewhat of a magician with a sewing machine."

"I agree," Amber said. "It's almost custom designed for you now, Mrs. Tucker."

"Well, that's why Kendall is our lead seamstress. She makes sure all the Diablo Designs fit our clients perfectly." Deena winked at Kendall.

"My granddaughter Lexi is very excited about her First Noel gown. I see some of the other debs are here today." Mrs. Tucker pointed at a few teenage girls gathered on the other side of the boutique. "I'm glad we've already selected her gown."

"It's that time of year," Deena agreed.

"Oh my. Look, is that Claudia Fine?" Mrs. Tucker said, her voice lower now. "It is."

The woman in question walked over.

"Claudia, so good to see you," Mrs. Tucker greeted.

"Wonderful to see you too, Patricia."

Kendall turned her head to see to whom Mrs. Tucker was speaking. A beautiful woman who looked more like she was headed to a formal luncheon than shopping on Black Friday stood on the other side of Mrs. Tucker. Everything about her screamed regality: from her black pantsuit, leather heels, and matching clutch to the tight chignon bun at the back of her head and her fierce red lipstick.

"I see you're like everyone else in the city. Getting some shopping done," Mrs. Tucker observed.

Claudia nodded. "A little."

Mrs. Tucker continued her questioning, as if she were interviewing Claudia for the society page of the newspaper. "I understand your granddaughter is living with you. She's sixteen, right? Will she be following the

Fine family tradition and participating in the First Noel Ball this year?"

Claudia shook her head. "She is with me, but no, she won't be a participant."

"Oh, I guess not, considering everything that's happened. My condolences to you and your family." Mrs. Tucker gave an apologetic look. "Maybe next year. The First Noel Society has been known to make exceptions for age, and you do sit on the board."

"Thank you, Patricia. It has been a tradition for years. However, in the grand scheme of things, I don't think she'll be the one to continue it for several reasons. The society has a reputation to uphold. I love my granddaughter, but I also recognize that she doesn't have the—how can I say it?—je ne sais quoi needed for such an esteemed event." Claudia sighed.

"Oh, I see." Mrs. Tucker nodded. "It isn't for everyone, but . . ."

"It certainly isn't, and especially not for young ladies who haven't been raised in a conducive environment and received the proper training to be a deb," Claudia explained. "And she recently lost her mother, remember. Beyond that, I firmly believe, just because you have the pedigree doesn't mean you're fit to wear the crown."

"Well, I mean, surely . . . ," Mrs. Tucker began, as if she didn't know quite how to respond. "Certain exceptions can be made, considering the circumstances. You know I'm on the board, and I'd have no problem making sure the application is approved. There's still time if—"

"We won't be seeking any exceptions," Claudia interrupted gently. "No need for that."

Kendall suddenly became self-conscious and felt as if she was eavesdropping on a conversation that she shouldn't be privy to hear, but there didn't seem to be the right moment for her to excuse herself.

"Well, welcome to Diablo's. How can we help you today?" Amber smiled.

"I'm looking for Deena Diablo, actually," Claudia answered.

"This is Deena." Mrs. Tucker immediately touched Deena's arm. "Deena, this is *Claudia Fine*." The way Mrs. Tucker said the name indicated how important she felt the other woman was.

"Of the Fine Foundation?" Amber asked.

"Yes," Mrs. Tucker said.

"Pleased to meet you, Mrs. Fine." Deena extended her hand, and Claudia shook it. "What can I do for you?"

"Well, I placed an order online a few weeks ago, but I realized instead of delivery, it's scheduled for pickup. So I'm here to pick it up," Claudia said.

"No problem. Come with me. I can help you with that," Deena said, taking her by the arm.

"Niya, I'll be back in a few moments," Claudia called as she and Deena began to walk away.

Kendall's eyes shifted, and she noticed a young lady in a black hoodie and jeans leaning against the far wall. She seemed to be so consumed with the cell phone in her hand that she barely looked up. Kendall looked over at Amber, who gave a simple shrug.

Claudia stopped in her tracks, gave a deflated sigh, then looked back at Mrs. Tucker. "Like I said, je ne sais quoi." Then she and Deena headed across the boutique.

Hold up. Wait. This can't be the granddaughter, Kendall thought. *There's no way they stood there and talked about her like that, as if she wasn't standing nearby*. If anything, the entire conversation they'd had moments before demonstrated a lack of class and demeanor, she decided.

Without hesitating, Kendall walked over to the girl and said, "Hi there. Niya, is it?"

"Yeah." Niya barely nodded.

"We actually have a lounge area where you can sit and wait for your grandmother if you'd like," Kendall offered.

"I'm good," Niya said, giving Kendall a bothered look as she stuffed her phone into the pocket of her oversized sweatshirt.

"Are you sure? There are some young ladies your age sitting over there. You don't have to be over here all alone," Kendall told her, pointing to the open area in the center of the store, where several teen girls had assembled. Some were waiting to try on dresses, and others were waiting while their mothers shopped.

"I said I'm good. Hopefully, we won't have to be here that long." She sighed and looked down at the floor.

"Kendall, you're needed for a fitting," Luigi announced over the sound of Bing Crosby's non-urban voice singing "White Christmas."

Had it not been one of the busiest days of the year and had she not already had a ton of work, Kendall would've stayed and talked with Niya until Claudia returned. But now wasn't a good time. It was obvious that the young lady was uninterested in moving, so Kendall gave up.

There's definitely something about her. Despite her nonchalant demeanor, this girl is special. I know it, she mused silently as she headed to the alterations room.

"Oh my God, I'm tired. Maybe instead of going home, we should just sleep here. There's no point in leaving, anyway," Amber said as she flopped dramatically onto the large cutting table.

Kendall looked up from the dress she was hemming and checked her watch. She'd been so busy that she hadn't even realized how much time had passed. "Is the floor clear?"

"Floor is clear and clean, and the chaos is over for the day." Amber placed her hand across her forehead.

"I can't believe it's this late." Kendall yawned. "Today has been a day, that's for sure."

"It has," Amber agreed. "We still hitting the mall?"

Traditionally on this day of the year, the two besties would be ready to walk out the door the moment the boutique closed and join the rest of the Black Friday shoppers. It wouldn't matter to them that they'd missed the doorbusters or early morning bargains. The only thing that would matter was that it was the first shopping day of the holiday season and they would participate. But this year Kendall didn't have that same sense of urgency. Something was bothering her, and she couldn't understand what it was.

"Uh, I don't know. I'm not really feeling it this evening," Kendall said.

"What? Why not? We always grab our Black Friday bargains, then go to dinner, so we don't have to eat leftovers," Amber whined. "And I'm starving."

Kendall began pondering whether she had enough energy to indulge Amber in their usual tradition. It had already been a long day, and they had to work again tomorrow.

Just then, Deena strolled into the large, open work space where Kendall spent most of her workdays. It held various sewing and serger machines, racks of material, and shelves filled with thread, buttons, lace, and anything else any great seamstress could possibly need to get any sewing job done. "Good. You're still here, Kendall. I need a huge favor."

"Uh-oh," Kendall said with a faux sigh.

"Can you drop this off to Claudia Fine for me on your way home?" Deena asked, holding up a small plastic bag. "I would take it myself, but I'm meeting some friends for dinner."

"What is it?" Kendall asked, curious about the contents of the bag that Deena held.

"Her glasses. She left them at the register," Deena answered. "She called, and I told her you live in that direction, so I figured you wouldn't mind dropping them off for her."

"Why can't she just come get them herself?" Amber asked. "Or just wait till the morning?"

The annoyance in the glance Deena gave Amber was obvious. "Well, maybe they're for reading and she needs them."

"It's fine. I can take them." The words came from Kendall's mouth so fast that they nearly took her by surprise. Driving fifteen minutes out of her way wasn't something she would usually agree to, but she felt inclined for some reason.

"Really?" Deena and Amber said at the same time.

Kendall nodded and stood. "Sure. I mean, I do drive that way to get home. This could be my first angel assignment of the season."

"That's exactly what I was thinking." Deena placed the bag in Kendall's hand. "Also, can you please lock up? Everyone else is gone."

Deena wasted no time hurrying out the room as quickly as she had entered it.

"Guess that'll be your second angel assignment," Amber murmured.

Kendall ignored Amber as she grabbed her denim jacket, along with her purse. "It's no big deal, Amber. Deena has plans, and she's right. It is on the way home."

"But what about *our* plans?" Amber asked.

"We can grab something after I drop off the glasses." Kendall put her arm around Amber's shoulders as they walked toward the exit. She hit the security code as she grabbed her keys.

"I can't believe she suckered you into doing this. The only reason she even asked is that it's Claudia Fine. Deena's about as scared of her as you are of Deena. I don't get it," Amber said.

"I'm not scared of anyone. I wish you'd stop insinuating that." Kendall closed the door with a little more force than she had intended, causing Amber's eyes to widen. Kendall gave her an apologetic shrug. "I'm just saying, you know that's not true. I agreed because it's no big deal. If it was, I would've said something."

Amber remained quiet as Kendall locked the door, and she didn't speak until they got to Kendall's car.

"You want me to pick up food from Magnolia's and bring it over? We can watch *This Christmas* and start working on plans for the party," she finally said.

Kendall nodded. "Apology accepted."

"Whatever," Amber retorted. "You might not be scared, but you aren't slick, either."

"What are you talking about?" Kendall asked.

"The holiday lights at the Fine mansion. Don't act like that's not part of the reason why you don't mind going over there."

Kendall couldn't help but smile. Her best friend knew her well. It wasn't her main reason for agreeing to take Claudia her glasses, but seeing the incredible light display was an added incentive for doing the good deed. But beyond the opportunity to do her first angel assignment of delivering the glasses and to see the holiday lights was also something more: the unshakeable feeling that this was something she was *supposed* to do for some unknown reason.